POWER RIDE

J. L. O'Rourke

Millwheel Press Ltd

Cover picture by Bethany Nehoff

First edition 1992, Current edition published 2013 by Millwheel Press Ltd
Eyrewell Forest
New Zealand

ISBN 978-0-473-25101-7 Softcover
978-0-473-25102-4 Epub

Acknowledgements

I would like to acknowledge the help received from the following people. Firstly, Tama Drum Company of Japan for their kind permission to use their company name. Also Detective Inspector Dave Haslett of the New Zealand Police for his information on New Zealand police procedures and Dr Martyn Buick for prescribing Kit's medication.

All the characters in this book are fictitious. No relationship is intended to anyone living or dead. The bread shop and Kit's house are likewise fictitious.

Kester (Kit) Simmons, drummer with the rock band 'Charlotte Jane', was out of beat. He was stressed out, starving and he thought he was going crazy. Then, with less than two weeks to go before a national tour, Kit's precious drums and one of the band members are found slashed to pieces. The keyboard player, Avi Livingstone, is missing, Kit has no alibi and, to make matters worse, the police suspect him of dealing drugs.

CHAPTER ONE

The weary-looking blond was not amused.

"Stop!" His shouted command cut through the sound pumping from the Marshall amplifiers, stopping his five fellow musicians in mid bar.

"Hold it!" The blond spun round to face the drummer.

"Kit, it's no bloody good, man. It's not bloody working. And it's not bloody good enough. What's with you, man? This is old hat! We've done it a million times, a dozen already today. You're always telling me you can do this number in your sleep; so sleep then, because today you sure as hell can't do it when you're awake!"

The man half-hidden behind the rack of shining black Tama drums moved both his sticks to his right hand, freeing his left to push a lock of long, sweat-dampened black hair back into place.

"I'm sorry," he said softly. "It's just... I'm a bit... um... I'm just not very together."

"We noticed."

"Look, can we take a break? I don't feel so good."

The blond shrugged and, as an answer, unstrapped his ageing Gibson guitar and propped it up onto a conveniently placed support stand.

"Why not? It certainly can't make this damned rehearsal go any worse."

Kester Simmons pushed the unruly lock of hair back into place again then unthreaded his long, lean body from behind his drums.

"I really am sorry, Danny," he sighed.

The blond replied with a savage glare.

"I don't want apologies, Kit, I want a drum beat. Damn it all, Kit, it just isn't good enough. We are hitting the road on tour in just over a week - ten days to be precise - and this rehearsal has been a complete bloody disaster!" Daniel Gordon was working himself into a mild frenzy.

Kester turned to walk away but Danny had wound himself up and continued his harangue.

"And another thing, Mr Simmons! If your 'not feeling too good' means what it usually does, you'd better get your act together and you had better do it damned fast. It's a long tour and we're not babysitting you through it this time. You had better be on deck all the bloody way!" His voice dropped to a malicious hiss. "Don't you forget for one minute, Kit, that we are running real close to not making this tour at all, and it's all your fault."

"Hey, come on now!"

"That's below the belt!" The keyboard player and the rhythm guitarist leapt simultaneously to Kit's defence.

"That was below the belt and decidedly uncalled for," the rhythm guitarist, Mike Kiesanowski, repeated himself. "We are slightly behind schedule because our bass player quit. That was not Kit's fault and we are getting mighty sick of you hassling him about it."

"Huh!" Danny snorted in fury and stormed off towards the coffee-making facilities at the other end of the old converted carpenter's workshop the band used as a permanent rehearsal venue.

Without acknowledging Mike's spirited defence of him, Kit dropped his drumsticks into his gear bag and headed out the door into the garden which formed the surroundings for both the rehearsal room and Kit's own quaint little settler's cottage. Once outside he leaned his back against the wall, took a couple of deep breaths, ran both hands through his hair in a sign of despair then began a methodical but unsuccessful search of his pockets for a packet of cigarettes. Finding none, he muttered an unintelligible curse and slid down the wall into a sitting position. A few seconds later another figure flung itself down beside him and placed an arm around Kit's shoulders.

"You okay?"

Kit looked at the concerned expression behind the gold-rimmed glasses that framed the keyboard player's face and gave a wan smile.

"I'm not great, but I'll live." His smile opened into the hopeful, innocent expression normally seen on spaniel pups. "Hey, you wouldn't have a spare cigarette by any chance?"

Avi Livingstone pulled a squashed packet of Rothmans from the hip pocket of his ancient, faded Levis. He flicked it open but it revealed only the tattered remains of a cigarette which Avi threw away.

"Sorry, Kit, that's it. How come you're scavenging again anyway? Can't you afford your own?"

"Um... no," Kit replied apologetically. "I'm broke."

Avi sat back and his soulful brown eyes subjected Kit to a long, searching appraisal.

"Look, Kit," he said eventually, "I know it's none of my business but was Danny's comment on the mark? I mean, you're broke already, and it's still early in the week, you say you're not feeling very well and, let's face it, your drumming's been half a beat off all morning."

Avi let the comment hang in the air but Kit declined to

answer, content to scuff the ground in front of him with the toe of his boot. Avi patted Kit gently on the shoulder.

"Come on, Kit, this is Avi. An honest answer, okay?"

Kit rounded on him, flicked Avi's hand away and snapped a reply.

"An honest answer? Oh yeah? And you're all going to believe me, just like that? I know what you all think. It doesn't matter what I say, you'll all believe whatever you damned well want to. And I suppose you'll be checking up on me with Gabriel behind my back."

"Hey, come on, calm down." Avi gently restrained Kit from getting up and leaving. "Calm down. I repeat, this is Avi you're talking to, not Danny, not Gabriel. I believe you. I always believe you. When have I ever not believed you? Come on, now, talk to me, what's wrong?"

"Sorry." Kit slumped back against the wall. "Honest answer? I'm broke because my money's been cut back again and I can't manage, not that I ever could. Mum and Gabriel said I got behind on the power and phone bills, even though I was sure that I'd been keeping up, so they've taken power of attorney over my money again. Gabriel pays everything for me and gives me a pathetically small amount of pocket money, which leads me back to my original statement - I'm broke!"

"Power of attorney? Can they do that at your age?"

"Oh yeah, you'd better believe they can! All my money is handled by them through a trust anyway, since I was in hospital last time, so I can't do anything about it - except grovel desperately."

"And you've been a naughty boy and spent your allowance already," Avi teased.

"Don't rub it in, it's humiliating enough."

"Sorry"

"Yeah, so I've got no cigarettes and Mum's out of town today so I couldn't phone her and hit her up for a loan - not that she'd give me money for cigarettes anyway. I'd just get yet another moralising lecture on the virtues of quitting. In answer to your other accusations, I know I'm drumming like an epileptic praying mantis but I'm not feeling very well and I don't feel well because I'm pretty stressed out. But it's just that, Avi, stress. I am not - repeat not - underlined, in capital letters not - stoned. Okay? Get that? Not stoned! Out of all of them, Avi, you should know I've been clean for over a year. You guys are as bad as Mum and Gabriel. They don't trust me either."

"Of course I trust you. I was just worried. Hey, if you're stressed out it's because something's bothering you. Can I help in any way? I'm here any time you need me, you know that. Do you want to talk about it?"

"Thanks, but no thanks. I'll be okay. I just need a cigarette."

Eighteen years of friendship had taught Avi when not to push Kit, so he backed off, lightening the tone.

"Tell you what then, why don't we leave Danny to cool off and sneak down to the dairy. I'll buy us a packet of cigarettes and we can share them."

"Um... I don't know when I can pay you back."

"So, who's counting? Leave it to me in your will," Avi grinned as he hauled Kit's lanky body to its feet. "Come on, before the pocket battleship launches another offensive."

By the time the two men had returned to the workshop

Daniel Gordon had left. The band's replacement bass player, Kelly Reynolds, their temporary backing vocalist, Joanna Greenwood, and Mike Kiesanowski were ensconced comfortably in three of the dilapidated arm chairs which formed a casual semi-circle around the primitive coffee-making facilities at the far end of the large room. Avi and Kit slumped into two of the other chairs, Kit completing the act by stretching his long legs out to rest silver decorated, black leather boots on the badly stained coffee table. Joanna lifted her tiny trainer-clad foot and kicked Kit's off the table.

"Get your feet off the table, you lanky slob!"

"It's my table," Kit argued petulantly, although he obliged, but only because Joanna had pushed his feet off and he couldn't find the energy to put them back on.

"So where's our beloved leader?" asked Avi, craning his neck to scan the room.

"He gave up on you lot, called you by all sorts of interesting descriptive phrases - especially you, Kit, then ordered a lunch break," Mike replied. "We have two hours of carefree liberty after which he expects us to perform - or else!"

"That wasn't how he phrased it," Joanna smiled.

"No, that's the edited version fit for human consumption."

"Great," said Avi. "So why are you lot still hanging around here?"

"We were awaiting your return to ascertain whether or not you wished to accompany us to luncheon."

Avi grinned at the young man who had given the pompous-sounding reply. Kelly Reynolds was a recent arrival to the group and was still somewhat of an enigma. Mike, Avi and Kit were founding members of the group,

'Charlotte Jane', and were old friends from way back. Mike had met Avi and Kit when the band was first formed; Avi and Kit went back even further, to their first days at Beckenham Primary School eighteen years before. Joanna, although new to the group, was a long-standing acquaintance. She was Avi's cousin and in the tight-knit world of their parent's religious community the two had grown up closely together. Danny Gordon wasn't a local by birth, but he had been around long enough to be considered part of the Christchurch musical establishment. He came originally from Geraldine, a small rural community south of Christchurch, but generally chose not to broadcast that fact too widely. Daniel Gordon had a serious self-image problem.

Kelly Reynolds, on the other hand, seemed eminently self-assured. He had a different style to the others. His short, trendy haircut and snappy fashion clothing contrasted markedly with the more traditional 'long-haired scruffy rock musician' image of Kit and Avi, and his way of speaking matched his style. It wasn't as if he was being consciously pompous either. Kelly came from an upper-crust Wellington family and had all the benefits of an expensive private school education. The accent came naturally, along with an eclectic knowledge of world affairs, an innate sense of style and, as Joanna had often noted, an elegant, almost balletic, way of moving. To Joanna's eyes, at least, Kelly was a very tasty package.

Kelly acknowledged Avi's grin at his accent with a slight bow of his head. He grinned back and continued, "Then the telephone rang for Kester."

Kit looked up, flicking the hair out of his eyes with a gesture that was so habitual it had been become almost subconscious.

"Who was it?" he asked.

"I'm afraid I don't know," Kelly shrugged. "He didn't say. He merely inquired if Kester Simmons, and he did use Kester, not Kit, was there. I said you had disappeared temporarily with Avrahim and that we had placed bets on the probable destination being the corner dairy. Fair guess? Anyway, I inquired if I could take a message but he declined and hung up. I'm afraid he failed to leave a name or a contact number."

He shrugged his shoulders expressively and stared at Kit whose face now registered a broad grin.

"Yes!" Kit shouted, punching the air with a fist. "Awesome!"

Joanna turned to Avi. "That makes sense to you, does it?"

Avi grinned and shook his head.

"No, but that's normal with Kit, he never makes any sense."

"Well, I have no intentions of playing guessing games, especially when I haven't been fed. To hell with you guys, I'm going to find some lunch. There is no way I am going to put up with any more of Daniel Gordon's little hissy fits on an empty stomach." So saying, Jo pulled an orange nylon parka from the back of the chair in which Kelly was languidly sprawled, thrust her arms into the jacket's sleeves and headed purposely towards the door.

"You know something?" Kelly said to no-one in particular, "The lovely lady has made an infinitely practical suggestion. Shall we join her?"

There was a general mumbling of agreement as the men rose to their feet and trooped out to follow Jo. As the party wended its way around Oxford Terrace, Joanna dropped back to fall into step with Avi.

"Cousin, tell me something. Kit's a bit out of it, isn't he? Do tours always have this effect on him?"

"Tours? No, they don't affect him at all, strangely enough," Avi replied thoughtfully. "Something is obviously bugging him, though. Mind you, that doesn't mean to say that it'll be anything horrendous. Kit doesn't have the most stable personality and he is apt to make monstrous mountains out of the most minute of molehills. Whatever it is, he doesn't want to talk about it. This, with Kit, means that it is probably something reasonably serious, but I can't force him to talk to me. I'll have another go later. I can usually convince him to talk, it's just a matter of easing him along gently. I can be very persuasive." He ignored Jo's expression of sarcasm. "I wouldn't worry about it too much, though. In the meantime, I would think the best thing we can do is keep Danny from ripping Kit's face off this afternoon."

"Danny doesn't like Kit much, does he?"

"Huh!" Avi's laugh was more a scoff of derision. "Rest assured, cousin dearest, it's nothing personal. This close to a tour, Danny hates everyone, including and especially himself. Tours might not affect Kit, but they blow Danny away. He'll get worse yet."

"Super." Jo did not sound as if she actually meant the superlative. "You mean we're likely to see some fireworks?"

"Better than Old Man Carson's bonfires. I guarantee it."

Joanna laughed and rubbed her hands gleefully. Then she stopped and looked serious.

"But Danny's such a little guy. He wouldn't be stupid enough to upset the whole band would he? Surely?"

"He would, he has and he will, no doubt, do so again. In case you hadn't noticed, Daniel Gordon is somewhat akin to your neighbour's crazed Jack Russell terrier. Wind him up enough and he'll tackle anything, even if it is three times his size. Mind you, we could have some real problems this tour. I don't think it's going to be a very smooth ride. Danny is still very angry about losing our last bass player and, even though we've got Kelly, Danny is determined to hold Kit responsible and to rub it in as much as possible."

"Why?"

Avi shrugged his shoulders and spread his hands wide in a gesture of genuine incomprehension.

"I don't know. Danny's just a creep, I guess."

"So why keep him in the band, if he's such a creep?"

"Two reasons, I guess. He's a damn good guitarist and vocalist and he sells records."

"Garbage! The band sells records, not Danny Gordon. 'Charlotte Jane' was selling records before Danny joined you guys, and who the hell was he? Some two-bit wanna-be from Geraldine! Come on, Avi, he might be a good guitarist but they're ten a penny. If the man is a jerk you've got to have a better reason than that for keeping him on."

Avi ran his hand thoughtfully over his unshaven chin. He shrugged again.

"You know something, Jo? I don't have a decent answer. I guess we've got so used to Danny being a prize prick we just take his temper tantrums for granted. I mean, nobody's perfect, and if we started throwing out band members who had personality problems there'd be bugger all of us left. Poor old Kit would be at the top of the list, he's completely scrambled, and I don't think I'm always the easiest musician to work with. Anyway, whatever Danny is, he's a good businessman. He's got a pretty watertight contract, so we're stuck with him for the duration, at least."

"The duration of what?"

"The cd, the tour and the next single. It could be an exhausting few months."

The group left the meandering twists of Oxford Terrace and strolled down Barbadoes Street to the small Avon Loop shopping centre. Kelly split from the rest and headed purposefully towards the health food shop, leaving the others to traipse their usual path to the hot bread shop.

Joanna was first to the counter, ignoring the jibes from the men as she ordered a sizeable quantity of cream and jam filled items. As Mike stepped forward to order a traditional mince pie, Avi pulled from his hip pocket a wallet as run-down as his clothes. From that he extracted a five-dollar note which he surreptitiously thrust into Kit's hand. Kit grabbed Avi's receding hand and squeezed it tightly in a gesture of gratitude, his smile a mixture of embarrassment and profound relief. Kit made his choice quickly but Avi dithered, staring up and down the trays of food. Mike checked his watch, raised his eyebrows expressively towards the others and shook Avi gently by the shoulders.

"Avi, can we dispense with the ritual daily guilt trip and just buy our bloody lunch?"

"Um..." Avi dithered some more.

"Now!" the others chorused together.

"Okay, okay, I'm buying, I'm buying." Avi dropped into a fake New York Jewish accent. "So I'm taking my time here, already. A man has to think about such important things."

The only response came from Jo. "Aaarrgghh!"

After another minute of dithering Avi finally purchased a couple of innocuous-looking scones and the entire entourage trooped back to the workshop, collecting Kelly who was waiting for them on the corner, clutching a bean sprout salad and a fresh orange drink.

When they arrived at the workshop, Daniel Gordon was waiting outside. His temper had not improved.

"Oh, joy to the world." he launched immediately into a verbal attack. "I really do have a band. Well, I have a ragged and motley collection of alleged musicians - whether I actually have a band is another question entirely."

For Mike Kiesanowski this, the latest of Danny's taunts, was the final straw. Tossing onto the ground the screwed-up remains of his pie's wrappings, he grabbed the diminutive lead singer by his shirt lapels and slammed him bodily back into the wall. By the time Kelly had prised the two guitarists apart, Daniel Gordon was sporting a cut lip, a bloodied nose and the makings of a black eye and Mike Kiesanowski was nursing bruised knuckles. Kelly let the beaten form of Daniel Gordon slump brokenly to the ground but he kept a firm restraining hand on the rhythm guitarist who was still shaking with anger.

"Cool it, you two!" Kelly ordered.

Danny made a move as if to argue then winced with pain and stayed put. Mike glowered.

"That's it!" Joanna, as usual, made the deciding move. "We call it quits. Right now. It's been a lousy day and if we attempt to carry on now, it's only going to get worse." She turned directly to Danny. "Look, mate, I don't know if you suffer from pre-tour nerves or whether you're always this obnoxious and I really don't care. Just get this through your thick head. You're no more indispensable than anyone else in this group. And you're not God. So back off. I might be the newest kid on the team but I'm not so desperate for work that I'm forced to take this kind of garbage from some up-himself little jerk with a machismo problem. Any more of these jumped-up little hissy fits of yours and you won't have a band, let alone a tour!" She turned back to the others. "Well, I don't know about you lot, but I've got better things to do. I'm going." She swung again to Danny. "We'll all be here tomorrow morning at the usual time. If you want to join us on this tour, be here but be civil. It's up to you. Think about it."

Without pausing to notice the expressions of shock and admiration on the faces of the men, Joanna thrust her hands determinedly into the pockets of her jacket and walked away. Avi was the first to break the embarrassed silence that suddenly descended over the men as they self-consciously avoided eye contact with each other.

"So, what now?"

Danny, who was still picking himself up tenderly from the ground, mumbled an oath which the others ignored.

"Well, without all the histrionics, the girl is right." Kelly took temporary charge in his clipped Wellington accent. "Continuing today in our present frames of mind would be counter-productive. Go home, people, do something non-musical and return tomorrow full of brotherly love and inspired genius. If you could just unlock the door, Kester, I will collect my Ibanez and be off."

"Wise move," Danny snarled. "You'd be a fool to leave it here."

Mike took two menacing steps towards Danny, forcing the

singer back against the wall for the second time.

"Don't start it, Danny, I mean it!"

Danny pushed him away.

"The man has a right to know," he sulked.

"Know what?" Kelly looked puzzled.

Avi stepped into his usual role of peacemaker.

"There is nothing to know. It's just one of Danny's little grudges. We got into the habit of leaving our gear in the workshop overnight. After all, it's all locked up and Kit keeps his precious drums there all the time. Anyway, your predecessor, Gary, left his bass there one night and found it the next morning with all the strings removed. Nothing serious. Just a bit bizarre. We still don't know how anyone got in and the police just wrote it off as some sort of silly prank."

Danny pushed forwards, dabbing blood from his face as he spoke.

"Oh, come on, Livingstone, don't be so wimpish! The police thought nothing of the kind, and you damn well know it. They may have decided to put that in their official reports but we all know what really happened, don't we Simmons?" He rounded on Kit who dropped his gaze immediately to his feet. Danny turned back to Kelly. "I ask you. The place is locked tight. Only two people have keys - Simmons and myself - and Simmons is crazy." Danny's tone became mockingly nasty. "Simmons also has a record with the police for taking too many happy pills, doesn't he? And an even longer record with the hospital's psychiatric ward. It doesn't take a Sherlock Holmes to figure out who tampered with Gary's bass - even if he was so spaced out he doesn't remember doing it."

"You have no proof of that!" Mike spat.

"Maybe not - but there's plenty of circumstantial evidence. Enough for Gary to decide he didn't want to work with Simmons any more."

"Well, it doesn't bother me," said Kelly lightly. He turned to pat Kit reassuringly on the arm. "Kester, I take people as I find them and I never pre-judge. Now, if you have the keys?"

Kit fished them out of the pocket of his skin-tight black jeans and handed them to Kelly without meeting his eyes. Kelly tried two of the keys on the ring before striking the right one, then swung open the heavy wooden door and disappeared inside the workshop, followed closely by Mike and Danny. They all reappeared in a matter of minutes, guitar cases in their hands.

"Tomorrow, ten o'clock sharp." Danny tried to sound as if he was still in control.

Mike threw him a mocking salute followed, behind Danny's departing back, by an obscene gesture as the three guitarists made their way down the driveway to their cars or, in Kelly's case, his bicycle. Avi shut and locked the workshop door then knelt to hand the keys back to Kit who had assumed an almost foetal sitting position against the workshop wall.

"Come on," Avi shook Kit gently, "Let's go inside." With long-acquired skill, he helped Kit to his feet and propelled him from the workshop to the back door of the cottage.

CHAPTER TWO

This time it was Avi's turn to sort through Kester's jumble of keys until he found the one which opened the back door of the historic cottage. Kit followed meekly as Avi led him through the small back porch. The porch had been an open space originally but had been roofed over at some stage before Kester took over the place; the ceiling and doors were simply too low to have been installed by anyone with Kit's nearly six and a half feet of height. Opening off the porch were three doors which, Avi knew from experience, led to the laundry, the bathroom and the house itself, via the kitchen. It was through this latter door he guided Kit, remembering just in time to force Kit's head down before his forehead and the door surround made brutal contact. Avi stored away the realisation that a normally-functioning Kit would have ducked the door automatically.

The inside of the cottage seemed out of context both with itself and its owner. Although Kit's own appearance showed a disinterest in his self-image, the cottage showed the obvious effects of fastidiousness to an almost compulsive degree. Not a single item was out of place and not a speck of dust was to be seen anywhere. As he led Kit gently through the kitchen area into the lounge, Avi looked around and shuddered. In spite of the extensive and beautifully crafted alterations, the cottage still felt to him more like a museum than a home. Avi sniggered to himself. Mike's wife, Sarah the psychic, would love this place, he thought. If any place was likely to be riddled with ghosts, it would be this one. Avi certainly never felt comfortable in it.

He propelled Kit to an oversized armchair covered in a chintz with an equally oversized and out-dated floral pattern, muttered some consoling words to make Kit stay put, then returned to the kitchen, which had probably been a separate room once but was now divided from the lounge by a wide, formica-topped breakfast bar in a very 1960s style. Avi knew exactly where to find things, so it didn't take him long to brew up two cups of instant coffee and return with them to where Kit was still sitting, staring vacantly at nothing.

The lounge was a large room which had been created by combining the two rooms on the left side of the house and the hallway which had previously run straight down the centre of the building from the front door to the back. Now the front door, an elaborately carved piece of kauri dripping in highly polished brass fittings, opened directly into the lounge. Two other equally ornate doors led from what had once been the passage into the cottage's only other rooms. The bedroom at the front of the house was now Kit's, although when he had first gone to live at the house, nine years before, it had been the very private domain of his grandparents. His room then had been the smaller, rear bedroom. It still contained a single bed, if it could be found under the stockpile of spare drum skins and other musical paraphernalia. It was the one place in the house that was never tidy.

Avi placed the rather-too-delicate china cups of coffee carefully onto coasters to protect the french-polished top of the carved nested table. In his own version of habitual gesture, he ran a hand over his angular, hawk-like features and straightened his glasses, mentally juggling the Kit who casually put his boots on the coffee table in the workshop with the Kit who polished antique furniture till it shone and who used bone china cups for coffee. As usual the different sides of Kester Simmons failed to come close to matching together. Just like the cottage. Antique furniture, cluttered Victoriana decoration and open-plan renovations. Perhaps the whole Simmons clan was crazy.

As he put down the coffee, Avi sized up the seating arrangements. He immediately regretted not sitting Kit on the couch where he could sit comfortably beside him, considered moving him, rejected the idea and settled instead for manhandling a matching armchair until he could sit almost in front of Kit, close enough to be reassuring but not so direct as to be confrontational. The psychology units he had thrown into his double arts and music degree had not been entirely without premeditation. He had handled Kit for a long time. He noticed that Kit was now starting to rock his body backwards and forwards. Avi frowned.

He reached out and put his hand on Kit's knee, creating contact. Kit raised his head to look at his friend but the gaze was expressionless. Avi smiled. Reassurance. With his free hand he smoothed back Kit's errant lock of hair. The contact was enough to get through and with a soft moan, Kit fell forwards onto Avi's shoulder, shaking. Avi held him close, surprised by the ferocity of Kit's responding grip. After a few moments Kit pushed himself away, sighed deeply and looked at Avi, red-eyed.

"I'm... um... I'm really sorry," he choked.

"It's okay. That's what I'm here for."

Kit got out of his chair and paced the room. He pulled a handkerchief from his pocket, wiped his eyes and blew his nose before flinging himself back into his chair and taking a long slug from his cup of coffee. Avi sipped at his own coffee and waited.

"Ignoring Danny," he finally broke the silence, "what's really up, Kit?"

"Nothing." Kit answered too quickly.

"Bullshit!"

"No, really, nothing. It's just Danny."

"Sorry, I don't buy that. You said earlier that you were stressed out. We can all see that you're stressed out. Sure, Danny's been picking on you but we've worked with him for three years now, we know he's an arrogant little bastard. So, logic says that something other than Daniel Gordon is the real problem. Right?"

Kit shrugged. "I guess so, yeah. Pretty much... um... well, no. Well, yes and no."

"I always did like your concise, clear, erudite answers."

"Sorry."

"Kit, nice and slow, from the beginning, tell me what's wrong."

Kit hauled himself from his chair again and began to pace the room in agitation.

"No. No... um... no, really," he spoke quickly in a desperate but failing effort to be convincing. "Honestly, Avi, everything's okay."

"You just admitted it wasn't." Avi kept his tone gentle yet inquiring.

"Yeah, well, um...," Kit floundered. "Look, Av," he tried again, "just forget it, okay? Look, yeah, I'm a bit stressed, but it's just a bad day, all right? Can we just forget it, please?"

Avi gave a long, unimpressed sigh and threw up his hands in surrender.

"Okay, have it your own way. Consider it, no, damn it, it's not forgotten, just ignored for now, okay? Don't lose it, Kit, there's too much at stake this time." He rose and went to his friend, guiding him to the couch where he sat beside him. He patted Kit's shoulder reassuringly. "Mike and I, at least, both know how much stress this tour is going to put on you. We're with you all the way, any time you need us. Use us, Kit, for God's sake, use us. Talk to us."

Kit shot Avi a reproachful glare.

"You don't think I'll make it, do you, mate," he spat, emphasising the "mate" into an insult. "Every single bloody one of you expects me to crap out. Kit, the junkie, might stay clean if he's kept nicely at home weeding the garden and feeding the ducks but wait till we hit the road, he'll fuck it up, yeah? Got a book running yet? Odds on how many days till I shoot up?"

"Yeah, sure, Kit!" Avi spat back, suddenly furious. "Why the hell not, we've got nothing better to do. Get a life!"

They sat for a few moments in a stand-off, glaring, before their anger died as quickly as it had arisen. Avi broke the silence first.

"Sorry. That was uncalled for." He laid a hand on Kit's knee. "No, I'm not expecting you to fuck up. I just know that you find it hard going sometimes and we all know how tough it is on tour. Actually, it's quite the opposite to what you were just thinking. Mike and I really expect you to come through this okay. That's the point I was trying to make. We've watched you go to hell and back and, oh hell, how do I want to put this, um," Avi searched desperately for the right words, "look, if you feel you're slipping backwards, especially when we're on the road, don't hesitate to use us as brakes."

He flashed Kit an apologetic grin which was returned immediately.

"Sorry," Kit reciprocated the apology. He grinned again, looking up under his hair with his spaniel-puppy impression. "Got a cigarette?"

"Sure." Avi hauled the packet from his pocket and lit two, passing one to his friend.

"Thanks." Kit drew hard, letting out the smoke in a long sigh. "It's not drugs," he said at last. "The problem. It's not drugs. I promise you that. I just..." he paused.

"Just what?" Avi prompted, knowing Kit would not continue without a push.

"Just, um... just I hope they won't have to be the only answer," Kit finished in a rush.

"Drugs never have to be the answer," Avi said gently.

"Huh!" Kit spat derisively. "They are though, aren't they, for me anyway."

"Not any more."

"Yeah they are. Think about it. I'm not a bloody ex-addict. There's no such thing. And if you look at it, I'm not even a clean addict. Just a legal one. There's only three things different between the heroin I was shooting up last tour and this," he hauled a small bottle from the pocket of his jeans, "this crap."

"Three things?" Avi was intrigued in spite of himself,

"Yeah." Kit shook the bottle and the pills in it rattled. "This crap is cheaper, I can't get arrested for carrying it around and it does no fucking good at all! But it's still junk, isn't it. I'm still a junkie. Shit, Avi, I've been a junkie since I was nine years old. I'm going to be on these bloody things for the rest of my life. Tell me again drugs aren't the answer. Dr

Phillips keeps telling me to keep trusting them, they're the only answer I've got."

"Dr Phillips is right. You're twisting the answers back to front and you know you are. For you, with your medical problems, those pills are the answer, sure. They get you through the day pretty much in one piece and that's a damn good achievement, but you know damn well I was talking about the illegal kind. There have got to be several alternative answers to any problem before you need to fall back on that one. So promise me that you are not going to do anything rash."

"Don't worry, I promise. Hey, I really do want to do this tour straight, you know. For one thing it'll be an education. I might finally get to see some of the countryside. I was so stoned on the other tours, all I've got is a few flashbacks of sheep and a hazy memory of a blond roadie in the flys of some theatre."

Avi's eyes widened.

"What blond roadie?"

"Um... I don't remember his name. I don't remember a damn thing actually but I think it was good."

"Yeah, well that's another thing you'd better watch out for this tour. It's a bloody miracle you haven't got A.I.D.S. yet. You play in both the high-risk groups."

"Yeah, yeah, yeah, and you've always been a bloody angel," Kit tempered the insult with a smile. "You used to go with heaps more groupies on tours than I ever had roadies and you straight guys aren't immune, no matter how many prayers you slip up every day."

Avi laughed good humouredly at Kit's small dig at his family's religious beliefs. Their friendship was founded on a solid enough base to allow free trade in minor insults and the fact that Kit had made the joke signified his black mood was dissipating. He decided it was a good time to change the subject.

"Another coffee?" he asked.

"Yeah. Why not?" Kit moved to turn on the electric jug. Avi collected the two cups and followed him into the kitchen.

"What blond roadie?"

"I don't remember," Kit laughed. "Maybe it was a sheep."

"No, that was Gary," Avi answered, deadpan.

"He's not blond."

"No, but his sheep was."

Kit laughed again, then turned and enveloped Avi in a hug.

"Thanks."

"Quite all right," Avi returned the gesture, unembarrassed. "What did I do?"

"Made me feel better. Maybe it's just Danny. Maybe he just gets right up my nose."

"No maybe, that's a bloody certainty!"

"Talking about Danny, or rather, seeing he's not here to interfere, can you tell me exactly what is going to happen in the bridge of that bloody song he was ranting about earlier?"

"Which rant in particular? Which song?"

"You know," Kit carried his now replenished cup back to the lounge and sat down. "The one about the welder and the dweeb."

"The what?" Avi was totally mystified. He had written every song in the band's set and Kit's description meant nothing.

"The welder and the dweeb." Kit repeated. "Well, that's

what the words sound like through my foldback."

Avi ran his hands over his stubble, thinking fast.

"How does it go?" he asked nervously.

"Oh, you know," Kit answered, "like this." However, rather than supply Avi with the melody, he reached forwards and tapped out a beat on the coffee table with his hands.

"Yeah, thanks. That helps a hell of a lot," Avi grinned.

"It's in A flat and has that walking bass intro," Kit tried again. Light dawned.

"You do well to dream!" Avi spluttered. "Welder and dweeb indeed! Christ, Kit, are you sure you're not sniffing something up behind those drums?" He gasped quickly as he realised he may have said the wrong thing, but Kit's mood had definitely improved and he wasn't taking offence. A second thought caused Avi to gasp again. "Could you really not pick up the proper words or were you having me on?"

"No." Kit's reply was serious. "But then I can't say I listen that closely. Not to Danny anyway. I've got Kelly turned up full in my cans and just enough of Danny and the rest of you so I can hear your leads and fills. Doesn't matter a damn to me what words he sings."

"Yeah, I think I'll ask the others though. I'd hate to think the punters out the front can't understand us. I spend a lot of time on those lyrics, they're supposed to be deeply meaningful." He sounded hurt but his glinting brown eyes made a lie of his expression. "So what did you want to know?"

"I'm not sure where Danny wants the stops. He's changed his mind about four times and now if I try to ask him he just shouts at me. Kelly seems as confused as I am. We're trying to follow each other and just end up spiralling up each other's ..., well, um, getting more confused. Have you got time to run over it a couple of times? I'd appreciate it."

"Sure, let's go out the back. I'll show you on the Roland."

"Great."

Joanna Greenwood whistled to herself as she strode jauntily down the Avon Loop towards the central city. She had enjoyed telling that jumped-up little jerk what she thought of him. Silly little twerp. Who the hell did he think he was? Joanna had very little tolerance for fools and none at all for arrogant ones like Danny Gordon. Telling him what she thought had put a nice edge on her day. She always liked a good argument, especially when she won.

Now, to top it all off, she had some hours up her sleeve to go shopping. It was time to find that elusive little number she had been seeking to take on tour: Something scarlet and revealing in all the right places. So what if her extremely religious parents would have a fit and call her a slut - they were never going to see it, she would make sure of that. Okay, so maybe she was being a bit daring. So what if her figure was a little too generous to ever land her a job as a fashion model, she was all in proportion and had legs that looked damned fine in a short skirt. At least she had something to put in it. So what if her penchant for cream cakes meant she would look like her mother one day, that was a long way off yet and, damn it, the mere thought of them made her hungry again. She was just debating stopping for a quick fix at the bakery when a car horn tooted beside her. She turned to find Mike beckoning from behind the steering wheel.

"Want a lift?" he inquired. "I'm going into town, I can take you as far as the Cashel Street parking building."

"Great, thanks." Jo accepted with alacrity and climbed aboard.

"What do you reckon we should do about that bastard?" Mike asked as he pulled back into the traffic.

"By 'that bastard' I have to assume you mean Danny? I don't know. I guess it's not really my problem, is it? I mean, I'm only on this tour to do back-up vocals, I don't have to live with him all the time, like you guys. I've got to admit though, polytech's going to seem really peaceful in comparison."

"Going back next year, are you?"

"Yeah, two down, one to go then I'll be Joanna Greenwood Dip Jazz or something. I don't think Mum thinks the jazz diploma is as fancy as darling-mister-super-perfect-cousin's double psychology and music degree, but I reckon it's every bit as hard to get."

"You've got a real competition thing going with Avi, haven't you?" Mike inquired.

"You noticed?" Jo laughed. "I've had Super Cousin thrown up at me all my life. It's a wonder I don't hate him."

"You've just decided to prove you're as good as he is."

"Of course I am, better probably. It's making them realise it that's the difficult part. Actually, I like Avi in spite of all the parental hype. But then I know a few of his vices."

"I'll bet you do!" Mike concentrated on his driving for a few moments than tried again. "Any ideas though? About Danny, I mean."

"Well, as I told Avi earlier, if the guy's such a jerk just get rid of him. No contract's that watertight, surely."

"My thoughts exactly. I've been giving the matter a lot of thought lately. I'm sick to death of the way he's been hassling

Kit. He's a nice guy really, Kit that is, and it's not his fault he's a bit screwed up. He's trying really hard and the last thing he needs is Danny flying off the handle at him all the time."

"So what are you going to do?"

"Well," Mike paused thoughtfully as he negotiated a corner. "Contracts. Use one contract to break another." He winked at Jo. "I'm off now to negotiate a deal with my hitman."

"Oh, right." Jo felt it was inappropriate to ask any more. Anyway, Mike was now pulling into a vacant slot in the car-park and preparing to depart. Jo did likewise, although preferring the lift to the stairs. Mike turned as he headed down the staircase.

"Jo," he threw back. "A favour. You haven't seen me since we left Kit's, okay? We haven't spoken."

Danny Gordon powered his huge car away from the rehearsal venue in a cloud of exhaust fumes that matched his mood. Faggots, the whole lot of them. Poncey, ignorant faggots. Great band, yeah right! A poofter, an upper-class twit and the bloody Bobsey Twins. And Kiesanowski. Bloody Polak. He would keep.

Crashing red lights and squealing the tyres on the intersections, Danny thundered the V8 monster out of the far end of the Loop onto Fitzgerald Avenue towards the gymnasium. Maybe if he pumped some iron for a couple of hours he could forget about those other wimps. At the thought of them he snorted derisively. Not a body between them. Simmons and Livingstone, pair of faggots, three inches wide across the shoulders if they were lucky! Danny flexed his own overly-developed shoulders, taking an almost sexual pleasure in the feeling of the seatbelt rubbing against his finely honed muscles. He might be short but it was a long, long time since anyone had dared make a joke about it.

He smiled as he pulled into the gymnasium car-park. He liked this place. He was somebody important here. Doubly important. He was Danny Gordon, famous rock musician. He was also Danny Gordon, champion power lifter. Young men looked up to him. Young women fell at his feet. Or so he believed. And judging by his reception as he walked into the building, he could have been right. Several equally well-developed young men did call out and wave greetings and two voluptuous leotard-clad young girls wasted no time in flinging themselves around his neck with ego-soothing cries of "Oh, Danny!". He thought again, fleetingly, of his fellow band members and allowed himself a self-satisfied smirk. Eat your heart out, Simmons, this is a real man.

Avi was guiltily disposing of the wrappings from fish and chips when the phone rang. Guilt was a normal by-product of food as far as Avi was concerned. His up-bringing had been unusual in an ultra-conservative, old-testament-based religion that was considered by outsiders to be a cult. To his father everything that was pleasurable was also evil and that included food with tasty fillings. In his head he heard his father lecturing on temptation and the road to hell. He secretly envied Jo's more lenient family who had a slightly wider view of what food was acceptable, and admired the way she could demolish a pizza and a cream bun with no qualms whatsoever. He also felt guilty about working on Friday evenings as Friday evening to Saturday evening was their holy day of rest so working on it was another of his father's roads to hell. But, no matter how religious his father was, Avi was a pragmatist. He had to be to remain a working musician. He knew his parents disapproved, but Friday and Saturday was when rock music was played and, as he had told his mother several times, even if there were enough weddings, birthdays and business conventions to keep him employed, he would go insane playing the boring covers they involved. And pragmatism at this time of the day in the present circumstances had demanded that Kit and himself be fed, so Avi had shelved his guilty feelings, yet again, and taken the path of least resistance - in this case, up Oxford Terrace to the fish and chip shop.

The phone's ring blasted over the cd playing on the stereo. Kit started, looked nervously at Avi to see if he had noticed, then reached forward to take the receiver with a shaking hand.

"Yeah?" he said hesitantly.

"Kit," the voice on the other end sounded cheerful. "It's Mike. I've got a fax here on my machine addressed to you. From someone signing themselves K.B."

"Oh yeah?" Kit was interested.

"Yeah. Says, and I quote, Deal finalised. First shipment due in eight weeks. Cash on delivery. Signed K.B. That make sense to you?"

"Yeah, thanks, Mike."

"So?" Mike was intrigued. "What's it all about?"

"Um," Kit hesitated noticeably. "I don't want to say at the moment, if that's okay? It's ... um... sort of secret."

"Secret, huh? It had better be legal, especially if you're going to use my fax machine as an address."

“Um…”

“Um what? It is legal isn't it?” Mike sounded sharp.

“Yeah, yeah,” Kit replied too quickly. “I reckon.”

“You'd better reckon right then. If this is some kind of bullshit, you'll be in more trouble from me than you've ever seen from Danny.”

“No, honestly, it's okay, it's just… I can't tell you about it at the moment.”

“You're giving out my fax number to someone who doesn't even sign their name, you won't tell me what it's about but I'm expected to believe it's okay just because you say so? Is that it?”

“Yeah, pretty much. Thanks, Mike. See you tomorrow.” Kit hung up quickly, his hand shaking even more. Avi returned from the kitchen bearing cups of coffee, one of which he handed to Kit.

“Secrets, huh? Arranging your love life?”

“No such luck,” Kit laughed. “It was Mike.” He offered no further explanation.

The young woman huddled on the edge of the tombstone, snuggling her jacket collar tightly around her ears to keep out the wind. She looked at her watch. Eleven thirty three. The lights in the little house over the river had been out for almost an hour. She would wait a while longer before going over. It was a bright night. And anyway, that other dude was still there. She had watched him arrive, looking up and down the street just as he always did. Why did he bother? He wasn't exactly inconspicuous, even if he thought he was. After all, she knew all about him but he'd never spotted her. None of them had ever spotted her. Not even Kester.

Kester Simmons woke with a start. Again. He groaned, ran his hands through his now tangled, sweat-dampened hair and squinted through the darkness at his watch. Three o'clock. He turned over, flung his face into his pillow and cried aloud.

"Please! Not again! Please! Just let me sleep!"

CHAPTER THREE

Avi was late. Mike had been early. Purposefully. It had nothing to do with being conscientious, or being in the least bit nervous about getting a blast from Danny for tardiness. It was curiosity. He had found Kit sitting in one of the huge armchairs, rocking gently, unshaven and bleary-eyed, his hands clasped together so tightly his knuckles showed white. Mike held out a sheet of paper.

"Here's your fax," he announced by way of greeting.

For several seconds Kit appeared unaware of his presence and continued to rock. Then just as the silence became so obvious that Mike considered speaking again, Kit looked up.

"Oh, hi, Mike. I didn't hear you come in."

"Here's your fax," Mike repeated, holding it out.

"Oh, thanks," Kit replied, but made no effort to take the paper. Mike gave up and placed it on the dining table.

"Are you okay? You look terrible."

"I don't feel so good."

"Should you be working today?"

"Well I'm sure not going to be the one to tell Danny that I can't."

"What's up? You didn't look too good yesterday either. You coming down with the flu or something?"

"Maybe," Kit grabbed at an acceptable answer, although he knew it wasn't the truth. "I'll be okay by the time we tour."

"Yeah, hey, do you want a coffee?"

"Thanks."

Mike moved to the kitchen, calling back to Kit over his shoulder.

"Say, I don't mean to be nosey, but what was that fax all about?"

Kit hauled himself from the chair and followed him into the kitchen, brushing his hair back as he walked.

"Sorry, Mike. I really don't want to say anything at the moment."

"Not acceptable. It's my fax machine. You owe me."

"Yeah, I guess," Kit admitted partial defeat. "I've been offered a chance to make some money, which I need real bad at the moment. But the guy who's running this thing, the guy who sent the fax, has told me not to say anything. If it gets out, I don't get paid. So I'm sorry, I really can't tell you. Not yet anyway. Maybe after I've been paid."

"Kit are you sure it's legal?"

"Um..." Kit stalled, thinking fast. "Well, I sure as hell don't want to go back to prison, and I'm too stupid not to get caught. Don't panic, your fax machine is safe."

Mike spun round, thrusting a cup of coffee forward like a weapon.

"Like I said last night, it had damn well better be. You involve me in anything daft and I'll make Danny Gordon look like a pussy cat, got that?"

"Yeah, I got that." He took the coffee with both hands but that still wasn't enough to stop the cup shaking violently. Kit placed it hurriedly on the breakfast bar and thrust his hands quickly into his pockets. Mike noticed but chose not to mention it. He tried a different approach.

"So who is this K.B. bloke anyway?"

"I'm not sure. Keith something. Barnett or something like that. I haven't actually met him."

"So how come he's got you doing a job for him?"

"He rang me. He seems to know me. Well, he knows who I am anyway. I have a funny feeling I'm supposed to know him but I can't remember. The name's familiar but I don't know from where."

"An old tour, maybe?" Mike hazarded a guess.

"Yeah, it's possible. It would certainly explain why I can't remember." Kit didn't offer the suggestions that had seemed to him even more likely, namely Paparoa prison or Sunnyside psychiatric hospital. He was having enough problems fobbing Mike off without adding to his concerns. "He's American," he finally added.

"Right," Mike answered absently, his mind more absorbed by the sound of Danny's V8 throbbing up Oxford Terrace. He cocked his head in the direction of the street, acknowledging the sound. "That's our cue for action," he said. "Let's grit our teeth and do it. And don't let the bastard get you down. You look bad enough already."

"Thanks a lot." Kit swallowed his coffee in two gulps and followed as Mike grabbed his guitar from where he had leant it against the kitchen cupboards and headed out the door.

By the time they had unlocked the workshop door, turned on the sound equipment, filled and turned on the old Zip and run a quick sound check they had been joined by Danny, Kelly and Jo. Jo turned on Avi's Roland keyboard and the three guitarists checked the tuning of their instruments against its pitch. Danny ran a fancy riff on his Gibson then swung it sideways on his hip to strike one of his carefully rehearsed lead-guitarist-sex-symbol poses. He aimed his first volley of the day at Kit.

"So where's your boyfriend then?"

Kit looked up blankly from behind his drums.

"What?"

"Your minder. Livingstone. Where the hell is he?"

Choosing to ignore the gibes, Kit shrugged, "I don't know," returning to the conversation he had been having with Kelly. "So the stops are at the end of bars three and seven, okay?"

"No problem. I'll watch you, so in case I forget, signal me in."

"Come on, you two!" Danny broke in again. "To hell with him, let's make a start. See if you've got your act together today, Simmons. We'll start with that one you ballsed up so badly yesterday."

Kit reached for his sticks with a sigh. Today could only get worse.

They were on their third number when Avi finally arrived. Danny, against all his own rules, stopped dramatically in the middle of a song.

"Well, well, well," he drawled slowly with venom. "What took you so long. Couldn't you find a nail polish to match your shirt?"

"Shut your face!" Avi snapped as he strode up to his keyboard.

Mike and Jo passed a raised-eyebrowed glance between them. Avi looked as bad as Kit. His angled face was unshaven but for Avi in the mornings this was usual. His family had a formal evening meal and the band knew that Avi's father required him to shave, shower and change before they sat down to eat, so Avi never bothered to shave before five in the afternoon. But under the whiskers Avi's tawny colouring was flushed, his normally limpid brown eyes flashed and his breathing was ragged. It was obvious he was very angry, so obvious that even Danny backed off.

"So?" Avi stood, feet braced, behind the keyboard and glared back at Danny. "You going to stand there all day or are you planning on playing something." He swept his glare around the others. "That was 'Two Doors Down' you were playing as I came in. Hit it! From the top!"

With Danny and Avi so obviously ready to square off, the rehearsal maintained an uneasy truce as the musicians worked laboriously through their set. The tense atmosphere meant the music was technically correct but totally lacking in any atmospheric punch. Danny didn't seem to notice and Avi, normally the first one to comment, didn't care. After two and a half hours Mike finally called a halt.

"Come on, you guys, let's take a break. I'm starving."

Danny threw him a frosty glare, slung his Gibson onto its stand, flicked off his amplifier and headed for the door where he paused to turn back to the others.

"One hour!" he ordered, then spun on his heel and left.

The remaining band members let out a collective sigh of relief. Kelly, who as bass player stood closest to the drummer, noticed Kit's hands were shaking as he laid down his drum sticks and dragged his hands through his hair with a look of exhaustion.

"Avrahim," the bass player, in his pompous accent, suggested as he put down his own instrument, "if you have any of those filthy cancer sticks available, may I recommend your giving one to Kester, he seems to be in some immediate need."

For the first time in the day, Avi smiled.

"He's not the only one. Come on, Kit, Rothmans on me!"

"Smoke them on the way," Mike joined the conversation

as they trooped outside. "Let's go get some food. I wasn't kidding, I'm starving."

"Where does Daniel go every day?" Kelly inquired as they left the driveway and turned left down Oxford terrace towards the shops.

"Down to the gym for a quick muscle flex," Jo answered. "A couple of bench presses and a cup of steroids."

"Pity he doesn't bench press his brain," Avi snapped sarcastically.

"Or put his brain under a bench press," Kit added with feeling.

"Which reminds me," Mike interjected, "What bench-pressed you this morning, Avi? You were somewhat testy when you arrived?"

"Yeah, well, let's just say it was a bad-hair day before I even saw Danny Gordon."

"Any domestic scandal your darling cousin should know about?" Jo inquired hopefully.

"Sort of," Avi admitted. "Just the usual shit. Mum's only just told Dad that I'm going on tour again, so he was doing one of his get-a-haircut-and-get-a-real-job-how-will-we-make-a-man-of-you hissy fits which, of course, he automatically follows with his those-friends-of-yours-are-a-bad-influence-especially-that-no-good-Simmons-kid rant and I'm afraid I didn't wait around to let him finish his final we-paid-all-this-money-for-a-good-university-education-why-are-you-wasting-your-life tirade. Then, just to make the day complete, my bloody car broke down on the Waltham overbridge and I had to push the bloody thing all the way to Moorhouse Avenue before I could get it started again."

By the time Avi had run out of breath, Jo was giggling.

"It wasn't funny," Avi said peevishly.

"No, of course not," Jo tried to smother a giggle with her hand and failed. Not that she had tried very hard. Avi launched a swipe at her shoulder but he was laughing as well.

"Heartless bitch," he smiled.

At the bread shop the routine repeated that of the previous day. Avi paid for Kit's food without a word said on either side although the light touch of Kit's hand on Avi's shoulder expressed profound gratitude. As they were collecting their parcels, the door's bell jangled indicating another customer. Kit ignored it at first but jumped nervously to attention at the sound of a woman's voice.

"So you see, there is infinite potential for capital gain," the woman, slim, middle-aged and power-dressed, was saying to her two Italian-business-suited companions. On seeing Kit she stopped right in front of him and looked him up and down with distaste.

"Hi, Mum," Kit said grudgingly. "Thought you were out of town."

"Huh!" was her only response before she turned back to the two suits and re-opened her conversation.

"The area does have some minor inconveniences," she began, throwing her son a look that would have frozen hell, "but on the whole it has a pleasant ambience and most of the home-owners are upwardly mobile." She threw another sideways glance to see if Kit was responding but he had already left and was striding back towards his house. Avi and the others had to run to catch him up.

"Slow down," Avi begged.

"Bitch!" Kit pulled up short and slammed his hand

violently into a telegraph pole.

"Take it easy." Avi put a restraining hand on his friend's back. "Don't worry about it. You know what she's like when she's working."

Kit turned to face Avi, rubbing his reddening hand.

"I'm sick of it, Av. I can't do a damn thing right as far as she's concerned. I don't think she's forgiven me for ballsing up that last suicide attempt."

"Oh, come on, Kit. She's not that heartless. She is your mother, after all. She just wants the best for you."

"Like hell she does. She wants the best for Gabriel. I don't matter a damn."

"Maybe." Avi didn't want to get into an argument, especially when he suspected Kit was right.

Danny prepared himself carefully for his entrance into the gymnasium. It was a cool day but he still removed his cheap plaid shirt and rolled the sleeves of his t-shirt up to his shoulders to reveal his upper arm muscles. As usual the t-shirt was specially chosen a size too small to enhance the spread of his chest, which he puffed out as he left his car. In the foyer he acknowledged the receptionist's greeting with a rehearsed tilt of arm and profile. He was joined at his destination, the cafe in the corner of the foyer, by another man, equally powerfully built although considerably taller, who carried a tin which he placed on the table between them as he took a seat.

"Here," Danny's coach pushed the tin forwards. "This should keep you going while you're away on tour. It's pretty powerful stuff but it should give you the edge you've been looking for. You've certainly made a lot of progress in the last few weeks."

"Thanks," Danny pulled the tin towards himself. "How much do I owe you?"

"Quite a bit," the coach laughed. "It's more expensive than the last stuff, but I think you'll find it's worth the extra. Don't worry just now, I'll put it on your book."

"Great. I'll settle that when I get paid for this damned tour."

"Okay." The coach checked his watch. "Look, I can't stop. I've put some instructions in with that. Just don't overdo it. Like I said, it's powerful stuff."

As the coach left, another bulky young man rose from a nearby table and sauntered casually past Danny.

"What's this?" he jeered, flicking the tin. "Don't tell me the precious champ needs some help? Too old, Gordon? Or just too weak?"

Danny spun on his chair to face the newcomer.

"Don't kid yourself, Junior. I'm still going to win the championships. You don't stand a chance."

"Oh no?" the young man retorted. "You're going to miss all that training while you're away being the big stage hero. You might be the current champ but I beat you at the regionals and I'm going to do it again. The title's mine, Gordon. You're finished!"

Danny didn't wait to watch the young man's impressive exit, he was too busy staging one of his own, complete with slamming doors and spinning tyres.

"So what is up with Danny," Jo asked as the five musicians made themselves comfortable around the coffee table in the rehearsal shed. "Has he always been this much of a pillock?"

"No," Avi replied. "That's one of the problems. Actually to start off with he was quite a nice guy. Believe it or not, he was a quiet, shy little chap when he first auditioned."

"Yeah," Kit added. "I used to like him. He only got weird when he started body-building, which was about a week after he started hassling me about being gay. I think he only pumps iron so people won't think he's queer too."

"Why does he go on at you about that," Jo quizzed. "I mean, it's stupid, nobody would ever mistake you for one of those."

Kit let out his breath in an amused snort.

"I'm not sure how to take that," he replied. "What do you mean, nobody would ever take me for one of those? Why not?"

"Well," Jo looked over the lanky drummer critically. "You don't look queer. I mean, you're not, you know, camp or anything."

"Do I have to be?" Kit's queried softly, his voice edged with a tired sigh. "No, Jo, I'm not camp. I don't have a limp wrist, I don't speak with a lisp and I don't mince along wiggling my arse. But I'm still gay. Does that bother you? Because it sure as hell bothers Danny."

"You do so wiggle your arse," Avi interjected before Jo could couch a suitable reply,

"I do not," Kit countered good humouredly. "And anyway, I didn't think you noticed my arse. I didn't think you cared."

"I don't."

The good-natured banter continued until they heard Danny return. With his arrival, the atmosphere reverted to the quiet tension of the morning's session and remained quiet until Danny called the song 'You do well to dream'. Avi, remembering Kit's interpretation of the lyrics, lasted half a verse before dissolving into laughter behind his keyboard. Danny slammed a power chord and spun around to face him.

"What's so damn funny?" he snarled but Avi had collapsed into a fit of uncontrollable giggles and didn't explain. Danny ignored him, attempted to start the song again and struggled through two more false starts, both thwarted by bursts of laughter from Avi. On their fourth attempt Avi finally controlled himself and the song progressed as far as the bridge before Danny once again stopped it in disgust. This time his wrath was aimed at the rhythm section.

"What the hell do you two think you're doing?" he roared. "I told you where I wanted those bloody stops. Didn't either of you two listen?"

"Sorry, Danny," Kit acknowledged. "I went over this with Avi yesterday especially. That's where he said the stops went."

"He said wrong," Danny snarled. "You put the stops where I want them, okay?"

"No!" Avi snapped out of his gleeful mood. "It's not okay. Kit and Kelly are right. You're wrong."

"Since when have you been singing this bloody song then?" Danny squared off.

"Yeah, well that's all you're bloody doing. Singing it. I wrote it," Avi snapped back.

"Why don't we...," Kelly tried to intervene but was stopped by Danny's shout.

"You keep out of it, Reynolds. You've got no bloody opinion worth hearing. If it was up to me you wouldn't even be in this band. Gary would be playing bass and it would be that jerk there who would have got the boot." He indicated Kit who immediately dropped his gaze to the floor. "You're a waste of space, Simmons," Danny continued. "A drum machine would be a damn sight more use. At least you could program it to do the stops properly."

Kit stared blankly at Danny for several seconds before hauling himself from behind his drums and fleeing from the room, dropping his sticks as he ran.

CHAPTER FOUR

"Shit!" Avi exclaimed to nobody in particular. He switched off his keyboard and followed his friend. By the time he reached the kitchen of the little cottage, Kit was already frantically searching the cupboards, dragging out small plastic bottles which he shook then hurled to the floor as he discovered they were empty. He was just about to unscrew the cap on one that rattled hopefully when Avi forestalled the movement by grabbing his wrist.

"No!" Avi ordered, twisting the bottle of pills from Kit's grasp and placing them in his pocket. "Come on, man, that's not the answer. You don't need them."

"I bloody well do," Kit practically sobbed. "Look at me, I'm a mess." He held out a shaking hand. "Danny's right. I'm a waste of space. Everyone knows that."

"Come on," Avi led his friend gently through to the couch and sat him down, draping his arm protectively around Kit's shoulder and talking calmly. "Don't let him get to you, Kit, he's not worth it."

"It's not just Danny," Kit admitted quietly. "It's me. Danny just happens to be right. I really am a waste of space. I'd be better off dead but I can't even get that right."

Avi couldn't think of any words that didn't sound trite, so he settled for pulling Kit forwards and hugging him hard.

"If it's not just Danny, what is it?" he asked gently when Kit finally pulled away.

"Nothing."

"Hey, we went through his yesterday and I didn't believe you then either. Come on, I know you too well. Tell me what's up."

"Nothing," Kit repeated desperately.

"And nothing has you running back for drugs you haven't wanted since last year? Sure! And I'm Father Christmas!"

"You'll think I'm stupid."

"No, I'd never do that. It doesn't matter what it is, Kit, if it's bothering you this much, then it isn't stupid, it's important."

"Maybe it isn't important. Maybe I am stupid."

"Kester! You are not stupid!" Avi leant forwards and shook Kit lightly by the shoulders. "Listen to me. You're a good guy. You're a decent bloke, you're an ace drummer and you're not stupid. Under pressure, maybe, but you're not stupid. Just remember that, okay? Now, let's start again. What's wrong?"

Kit sighed deeply and rested his head on his hands.

"I think I'm going crazy," he stated.

Avi waited for him to continue. He didn't.

"Danny thinks you've gone already," Avi prompted gently.

"Yeah, but Danny's a prize prick! No, really crazy. Full men-in-white-coats, they'll-never-let-me-out-again type crazy. And do you know what really scares me? I can see it happening and I can't do a damn thing to stop it." Kit reached out and grabbed Avi's hand in both of his. "Avi, I'm scared stiff."

Avi returned the grip reassuringly.

"What about your psychiatrist? Have you been to see her?"

"Yeah, a couple of times, and I've done everything she said but it hasn't helped. It's not the same as the other times, that's what scares me. Well, it is and it isn't. Um... well, it's sort of like the other times but not quite. There's something really not right and I don't know what to do."

"How is it different, Kit? Think it through slowly. Take your time."

Kit rose and began to pace the room. Avi took two cigarettes from a fresh packet in his pocket, lit them and handed one to Kit who drew on it with obvious gratification. He pulled himself together in a conscious effort to be coherent.

"Okay. I've had two nervous breakdowns, as you know only too well, and another couple of near misses. The pattern has always been the same. Normally my bio-rhythms, or whatever they're called, go all to hell and I can't sleep. But that's usually fixed by medication. This time, instead of being awake at all hours of the night, I'm dog-tired. I'm so desperate to get to sleep it's a wonder I can stay awake to drum, but as soon as I get to bed I wake up again. Sometimes two or three times a night. It's driving me nuts. It's getting to the stage where I'm afraid to go to sleep because I know I'll just get woken up again. I've tried pulling the phone out of the wall a couple of times but then I forgot to put it back and I got yelled at by Gabriel and by Danny."

"Woah! You've lost me." Avi butted in. "How is pulling the phone out of the wall going to make you sleep better?"

"It isn't. I know it isn't. But I can't think of anything else to do."

Avi still looked blank.

"Well, I keep thinking I hear it" Kit explained. "That's what wakes me up."

Avi paraphrased to marshal his thoughts.

"You keep waking up because you think you hear the

telephone ringing?" he asked.

"Yeah."

"Sometimes two or three times a night?"

"Yeah."

"Is it ringing?"

"No. Um... well... I don't think it is. I don't know."

"Have you told your psychiatrist this?"

"Yeah."

"What did she say?"

"She thinks I'm heading for another breakdown. Just with different symptoms. Well, put it this way, she tells me that she thinks I'm heading for another crisis and that, with the right help, I can sort it out before things get too bad. I may as well tell you now, she doesn't want me to do this tour. I'm still going," he hastened to add, "she just doesn't want me to go. Mind you," he added, "that's not what she's told Gabriel. I'm not supposed to know this but Mum let slip that Gabriel had said that Doctor Phillips had told him that she thinks I might be developing schizophrenia, or something."

"Kit!" Avi sounded alarmed. "Is she sure? I mean, hell," He was lost for words.

"It's okay." It was Kit's turn to sound reassuring. "It had to happen sometime, I guess," he said philosophically. Kit smoked the rest of his cigarette in a few hard drags and threw the butt into the open fireplace. He continued. "And I'm losing things. I know in my other breakdowns that my brain has switched off, but that only happens in the final crisis. I get more and more hyped up until my brain shuts off and I'm bundled off to hospital. Why am I telling you this, anyway? You're the poor bastard who has to scrape me off the floor. I don't remember any of those trips to hospital. I just wake up there. But now I must be shutting off in sections, or something, and that scares me senseless. What if I shut off when I'm driving the van? I could kill myself - or someone else."

"How exactly are you shutting off?"

"Stupid little things. You know how I like to keep this place - it may look cluttered but they're all Grandma's things. I know exactly what is here and where everything is. And I always put things back exactly where they belong. I guess Grandma drilled that into me so well I haven't lost the habit. But lately I'll put something away and when I want it again it's either somewhere else, where it shouldn't be, or it has disappeared entirely and will turn up again a couple of days later, exactly where I first left it. Things... you know... without brains," he struggled for the right word.

"Inanimate objects," Avi supplied.

"Yeah, thanks, inanimate objects... don't move by themselves and I don't believe in ghosts, so I must be moving the damn things myself. I just don't remember doing it. Avi, Danny was probably right. I probably was responsible for the damage done to Gary's bass - I simply don't know."

Kit threw himself back into a chair, leant forwards and grabbed Avi's hands.

"Help me, Avi, please. I haven't had any real sleep for two weeks and I'm desperate. What am I going to do? How the hell am I going to make this damned tour?"

Avi moved to sit on the arm of Kit's chair. He put his arm around Kit's shoulders.

"Don't worry. We'll take things one step at a time. I'll give you all the help I can. We all will."

"Except Danny."

"Except Danny, agreed, but to hell with him. Forget Danny. Worrying about his reaction is only going to double your own stress load and halve your ability to cope. Leave Danny to Mike, I think he'll get the message across." Avi grinned. "We, on the other hand, are going to implement the Kester Simmons revival plan, stage one."

"Oh yeah? What's that?"

"To begin with, we tell Danny to stick the rehearsal and take the rest of the afternoon off. We take a stroll in the Botanical Gardens, peruse the art gallery and the Arts Centre, take afternoon tea at the museum. All the stuff you hate, Kester, fresh air and exercise. To be followed later by a visit to a friend of mine who has a magnificent sauna and spa complex to which I have access any time I like. The object of all this is, of course, to make you so relaxed that you will sleep like a little baby."

"I like it already. What's stage two?"

"How the hell would I know? Get your jacket."

Avi got to his feet and headed towards the back door, followed by Kit who paused in the kitchen to grab from a peg behind the door a black, nylon jacket inscribed with the Tama drum company logo. By the time Kit had donned the jacket and locked the house, Avi was waving cheerfully to a furious-faced Danny and gunning the motor in his disreputable-looking Toyota.

In spite of Avi's jibe about Kit hating fresh air, he enjoyed strolling in the gardens. No matter what the time of year there was always a profusion of greenery to revel in. Kit loved nature; that was one of the reasons he liked his little cottage. A quarter acre section with an established garden, butted against the bank of the Avon river, Kit's idea of perfection.

The museum and the art gallery were not places Kit would choose to frequent by himself, but Avi was an educated, erudite and interesting tour guide and Kit was fascinated in spite of himself. The neo-gothic quadrangles of the Arts Centre were, as usual, a bustling hive of colour and sound. They wasted a good hour there jamming on African instruments with a group of touring players.

Refusing to let Kit even glance at the bills, Avi then paid, not only for a slap-up meal at a well-known family restaurant - great food in a casual, relaxed atmosphere - but also for a supply of groceries as Avi had sneaked a look in Kit's pantry and found it not just depleted but completely bare. The middle hours of the evening were then spent in absolute and unabashed hedonism. Avi's friend was a university professor and his Ilam home had been created with no expense spared including a sauna, a spa and a heated indoor pool. The owners were involved in their own pursuits and happily gave Avi and Kit unhindered, private use of the lavish facilities. Kit asked why Avi had never taken him there before.

"I've never come here myself," Avi answered. "Well, I have been here a couple of times, obviously, or I wouldn't know the place existed, but they've been university staff parties." Avi looked embarrassed. "I've never actually used this place," he gestured around the pool complex, "it's not really my scene. Honestly," he looked even more embarrassed, "I had thought of coming out here a couple of times and inviting you, but, well, I never had the courage to do anything more than think about it, until now. I mean, you know what Mum and Dad are like, they're so conservative about modesty and all that stuff and, in spite of the vast trappings of wealth, the owners of this place are very straight."

"Oh! Right," Kit nodded in understanding before sinking back into the warmth of the bubbling spa waters.

Avi lay back in the spa and considered both his friend and the situation. If it was possible to lose weight from a frame that held none to start with, Kit had lost weight. A long, skinny, gangling character at the best of times, he now looked gaunt. Without the ever-present black t-shirt, black jeans and black boots, Kit was all hip bones and ribs and Avi had noticed with consternation that the normally skin-tight jeans sat with room to spare.

Avi looked from Kit's tall, slim frame to survey his own and grinned at the comparison. He didn't need his glasses to confirm his own summation made several years before that "Avi" was short for "average". At five foot eleven inches, he was average height for a New Zealand male, with an average build to go with it. His hair was an average mid-brown, although he did have to concede that the amount of length and curl would have been considered average only on a woman. Avi sniggered to himself. He was well aware that if it wasn't for the charisma gained from being a member of a successful rock band, he would at best be labelled as forgettable.

By ten thirty paradise for Kit was a warm bed and a pair of strong hands. Avi had been playing the piano for twenty years. His hands were ideal for the purpose - long, slender, strong and supple. Ideal, too, for giving massages which was exactly what, at ten thirty, he was doing to Kit. The combined influence of the food, exercise and relaxation eased the tension from Kit's strung-out body and he descended softly into much-needed sleep. Avi smiled down at the sleeping figure, covered him with a feather-filled quilt and crept from the room, flicking off the light as he went.

Out in the lounge, Avi wiped the surplus massage oil from his hands onto his jeans. The relaxation he had foisted on Kit had worked the same magic on him. Now all he wanted to do was sleep. His own bed would have been very welcome but he had promised a distraught Kit that he would stay and be there if Kit woke in the night. He opened the door to the spare bedroom, took one look at the amount of junk piled on the spare bed and shut the door again. He shrugged. The couch looked comfortable. He had slept on worse and, no doubt, would do so again. At least it was a warm night. Avi made himself comfortable and was asleep in a matter of minutes.

Four hours later the telephone rang. The phone sat on an oak sideboard, beside the couch on which Avi slept, but just out of his reach. The bell was loud and Avi was awake instantly. The telephone rang just twice then stopped. Just before Avi picked it up.

Angry, he slammed the receiver back onto its recharger and drummed his fingers thoughtfully against the sideboard. So, maybe Kit wasn't so crazy after all. Kit! Hell! Avi strode to Kit's bedroom and looked carefully around the door. He needn't have worried. Kit was still sound asleep, oblivious to everything. Avi closed the door and left him in peace.

"Sometimes two or three times a night." That's what Kit had said. Avi gave up on sleep. He made himself a coffee, scavenged around in the spare room until he found a rug, wrapped the rug around himself and settled onto the couch with the phone on his lap. Next time he'd be ready. He checked his watch.

The second call came an hour later. This time the advantage lay with Avi. The phone had not even completed its first ring when Avi snatched up the receiver.

"What do you want?" he snarled.

There was the faintest hint of a gasp of surprise before the call was disconnected. Avi was furious. Why would anyone pull this kind of cruel prank? And why pick on Kit? A crazed fan? Danny would love that. That was all the band needed right now. Avi yanked the telephone cord from its wall socket then spent the rest of the night pacing the floor in anger.

By eight in the morning Avi had chain-smoked an entire packet of cigarettes. He was tired, scratchy, uncomfortable and in need of a shower. And that was after only one night. No wonder Kit was freaking out in such a big way. As he stubbed out his last cigarette and added its butt to the mounting pile in the nearest of a curious collection of brass animal-shaped ashtrays which were conveniently placed around the room, Avi realised he was hungry.

Before heading to the kitchen he checked on Kit who was still asleep, a long, slender arm cradling his pillow over which his long, black hair draped in an untidy mass of ringlets. Avi retreated but didn't close the door this time. Kit would have to wake soon anyway, so there was no especial need for quiet on Avi's part. In fact, Avi decided, a bit of cheerful noise might be in order. He flicked on the radio, which Kit kept permanently tuned to the nostalgia rock station, and set about creating a breakfast of scrambled eggs on toast for two from the supplies he had bought the day before, singing along to Daddy Cool's classic 'Eagle Rock' as he worked.

Kit was awake when Avi re-entered his bedroom with a flourish, bearing two plates and two cups of steaming coffee with the practised confidence gained from years of holiday jobs waiting on restaurant tables. As Avi laid the meals down on the bedside cabinet, Kit sat up and hurriedly pulled on one of his trademark black t-shirts emblazoned, like his jacket, with a Tama Drum Company logo. He stretched languidly and asked Avi the time.

"About a quarter past eight. Have a good sleep?"

"Oh yeah, brilliant. I needed that. Sorry to have wasted your time though, Avi. But you see what I mean? I'm going mad. It's all in my head. As you witnessed last night, no telephones - just the ones in here." He tapped the side of his head ruefully.

Avi sat himself on the side of the bed and looked straight at Kit.

"That's where you're wrong, Kit. You're not crazy, at least, no more than usual. That bloody phone rang all right. Twice. Before I ripped it out of the wall. Speaking of which, I'd better plug it back in." Avi sprinted from the room, replaced the phone's plug back in the wall socket and returned, accepting the plate of food which Kit pushed at him as he settled back onto the bed. Kit regarded Avi thoughtfully.

"Run that by me again - real slow. You say the phone actually rang? Honestly?"

Avi ran a hand in a contemplative gesture over the stubble on his chin. He really did need a shower.

"Honestly. At two thirty and again at three thirty. Almost exactly an hour between calls. Kit, damn it all, whatever's happening here, I don't think it's very funny. I don't know who's making these calls but I think we should call the police."

"Are you sure?"

"Yeah, I'm sure."

Kit sighed and flicked the hair out of his eyes.

"Okay, I guess you're right. If they really are phone calls and not just figments of my increasingly demented imagination, I guess we should call them." Kit hesitated. "Um, Avi, will you make the call, please. I don't think they'll listen very favourably to me. I don't have a very good track record with them, remember?"

"Sure." Avi patted Kit reassuringly on the shoulder. "Come on, eat your breakfast before it gets cold." Avi chuckled. "I'll tell you one thing, though, whoever it was, I think I gave them one hell of a fright."

"Yeah? How?"

"That second call. I was waiting for it. Lightening fast reaction, if I say so myself. Scared the shit out of the caller. At least I think that was the reaction. I heard a gasp then the phone was slammed down in my ear - very quickly."

"Do we need to call the police then? If you scared him enough, he might not call back?"

"Get real, Kit! If there's even half a reason for these calls, whoever's making them isn't going to stop. And, by the way, who says it's a he? Crazies come in both sexes, you know."

"Yeah, I guess you're right, as usual." Kit hauled himself out of bed and into the black jeans and silver decorated black boots that he had dropped in a heap on the floor several hours before. "So what do I do next, Avi? I don't know how to cope with this."

"Well, like I said before, we start by calling the police.

They'll know exactly what to do."

"But I've got a record!"

"Oh, Kit!" Avi sounded exasperated. "Don't worry so much. It's a very short record, Kit, you're not exactly a hardened criminal. And it's got nothing to do with this. You're not the culprit, you're the victim!" Avi walked around the bed and gently sat Kit down on it. "Calm down. Just take it easy. I'll handle it. Look, yesterday you were all stressed out because you thought you were hearing things. Now we know this is real, don't, for goodness sake, get stressed out on things that are not relevant. Any dealings you've had with the police in the past are not the issue. They won't be mentioned. Trust me, okay?"

"Okay."

CHAPTER FIVE

On the southern side of Christchurch city, under the shadow of the exclusive Cashmere Hills, in the elegant dining room of the Greenwood family's Heathcote Helmore designed two-storey house, amid the dark-stained walnut furniture and the Rodd silverware, Joanna Greenwood was shouting at her father. Everything was normal.

"No!" She thumped both hands hard enough onto the table to make the cutlery jump. "For the umpteenth time, I don't know. How would I be expected to know? What is it with you people? I'm not his keeper, all right? He was at rehearsal yesterday. He will be at rehearsal today - he'd better be or Danny'll kill him. What he does in between is none of my business. He's my cousin. He got me a job in his band. That's all! I don't know what he does. I don't care what he does - or who he does it with! So don't bother asking me again!"

Joanna stormed out of the house, pausing in the oak-panelled hallway to snatch her jacket from where it hung over the stair rail.

"And another thing," she yelled back up the corridor. "You can quit all those hopeful little chats I know you have with Uncle Jacob. I don't care how good a match you think it would be, and what biblical precedence it might have, he's my cousin, it's a sick idea and I'm not marrying him! Ever!"

Jo slammed both the front door and the gate just to make sure they got the message, then grinned to herself as she strolled off towards the bus stop. It was a daily ritual. Her parents always had to make an issue out of something over breakfast. Her two younger brothers had figured out the answer, they skipped breakfast altogether, but Jo liked her food and, to be perfectly honest, she wasn't averse to a decent argument either. It was a good warm up to dealing with Danny later.

The sight of the 'Big Red' bus approaching forced Jo to sprint the last few metres to the bus stop, then, as the bus was full, she spent an uncomfortable journey squeezed beside an extremely obese woman who smelt badly of sweat, who wheezed and coughed and who rolled her own cigarettes with nicotine-stained fingers - in spite of the 'no smoking' signs plastered all over the walls of the bus. Jo closed her eyes and winced. This could be the start of a really bad day.

Jo practically fell down the steps of the bus in her hurry to leave it. She still had to walk about four blocks to reach Kit's house but the street followed the meandering track of the Avon River along one of its more picturesque settings, so it was always a pleasant journey. It was one of the oldest areas of the city - a tiny suburb of tiny settler's cottages, most of them like Kit's, lovingly restored and maintained. The accent was on colourful paint and a profusion of wrought iron. A nice place to live if you could afford the rapidly escalating land prices. Jo made up her mind to ask Avi how Kit could afford to own a house there. Lucky bastard!

As she had been making this walk every morning for three weeks now, she was on speaking terms with some of the other regular users. She bade "good morning" to the old woman feeding the ducks, to the grey-suited businessman walking briskly towards the city centre, to the strange woman in the spotted tights who wandered the riverbank with a dowsing crystal, to the young mother hustling her brood to school and especially to the two handsome young joggers. She was in a good mood again by the time she reached Kit's wisteria-covered cottage, but that wasn't going to stop her ripping strips off her cousin when she got her hands on him. Which was about now, she thought, as she recognised his car parked in Kit's driveway.

"Breakfast," she said out loud, rubbing her hands gleefully. "Second course."

However, if Avi Livingstone was to be Joanna's extended breakfast, he didn't seem overly concerned at the prospect. In fact, it took Jo quite some time even to find him. Her first move was straight to the rehearsal room, but it was still locked so she tried the house. The back door was open and Jo let herself in. Even then there seemed to be no-one about. Jo was about to let herself out again when she heard Avi's distinctive laugh coming from the small back bedroom. She looked around the door to see Avi, Kit and Kelly squatting on the floor in a rough circle around a pile of photographs. Avi handed the photograph he had been laughing at to Kit, who promptly moaned in embarrassment and thrust the photograph into the centre of the pile before Kelly could reach for it. Jo took a step into the room, put a foot against Avi's shoulder and pushed.

"Where the hell have you been, you stupid bastard?"

Avi crashed sideways into Kit who grabbed him to stop him falling any further, swung his legs around so that he was now sitting on the floor and straightened his glasses. He looked at Jo with genuine surprise.

"What the hell are you talking about?"

"You! I'm talking about you. Where were you last night?"

"What is this? The Spanish Inquisition? Where the hell

was I supposed to be last night and what the hell has it got to do with you? Since when have I had to report my every move to you, cousin dearest?"

"Look here, Avrahim Livingstone, personally I don't give a rat's arse what you do - but your mother does and your father does. And when you don't arrive home they assume all sorts of horrific scenarios for their darling baby boy. Then your father rings his sister who, as you well know, is my mother. And then she imagines all sorts of horrific scenarios and she hassles my father who, in turn, hassles me! Understand now? Ring your mother!"

"Hell! Mum! You're right." Avi leapt to his feet. "Sorry, Jo, I'll phone her now. Look, Jo, do me a favour. I stayed here, with Kit, but I don't want my parents to know that, okay? I'll ring Mum and tell her that I was too drunk to drive so I stayed at a friend's house. Just stick to that story and don't say it was Kit's. Please."

"What's the big deal? Why can't you just be honest and say you stayed here? What's wrong with Kit?"

"Do as he says, please, Jo," Kit intervened. "I understand." He grinned self-depreciatingly. "I'm not acceptable."

Jo realised what he meant. "Oh, right. Ok, Avi, what's it worth?"

"A cream bun for lunch."

"And a chocolate eclair?"

"All right. You drive a hard bargain. And a chocolate eclair."

"Done. But I won't lie. I'll just say that you turned up on time for rehearsal. End of story."

"Thanks, you're a life saver."

"If that means I've got a hole in the middle, thanks for nothing. Anyway, don't thank me, just pay up."

Avi had already picked up the phone and was dialling his home number. Jo turned her attention to the pile of photographs in the centre of the floor. She sat in the space vacated by Avi and reached for a snapshot.

"So what were you guys laughing at?" she asked.

"Old band photos." Kit rummaged through the pile and handed one to her. "Get a load of this one."

"Oh wow! When was this taken? You all look so young. Bloody hell, Kit, you didn't really wear those clothes in public, did you?"

Kelly moved to look over Jo's shoulder.

"Well, I recognise you, Kester. The drum kit has grown bigger and the hair longer but you haven't changed much. And Avrahim. The keyboard gives him away, even if the glasses don't. But I must admit he has aged more than you, Kester. Avrahim looks more, shall we say, lived in than yourself these days."

"I have to agree," said Jo, who was actually concentrating more on the feel of Kelly's breath on the back of her neck than on the photograph. "Avi seems to have changed more than you have."

"Nah!" Kit shook his head. "It's all relative. It's not that, at twenty three, Avi looks older, it's more that, at seventeen, he looked seventeen."

"Say that again in English."

"Sorry. It's simple. At seventeen, Avi looked seventeen. He was just finishing his final year of high school. You know Avi, straight-A student, university course planned, no problems. On the other hand, going by the date on the back of that photo, I had just got over my second nervous breakdown. The photo says September so it must have been taken three months after I was released from Sunnyside hospital. I was on medication up to my eyeballs, and probably a few other things as well. So you see what I mean. Avi has grown up, he looks older now because he is older. I've looked this haggard for years."

Jo didn't know how to answer.

"Have you two known each other for a while then?" Kelly inquired.

"Oh yeah, years. Eighteen years, actually. I met Avi on my third day at Beckenham Primary School. He saved me from being pushed around by some bigger boys and he's been acting as my guardian angel ever since."

"So Avi's the elder of you two, then?" Jo asked. "I've wondered about that."

"Yeah, but only by two and a half weeks. Seventeen days to be precise."

Kelly pointed to another figure in the photograph. "Is that Michael?"

"Yeah."

"Now he does look older."

"So he damn well should, he's fathered three children in the mean time."

"Busy man."

"Yeah. Mind you," Kit added, "He's older than us to start with."

"Who are the others?" Jo asked.

"Dave Kilpatrick on bass and Peter Branston on lead guitar. They've both gone to Australia. Dave was replaced by Gary, who was your predecessor, Kelly, and Danny took over from Pete three years ago."

They were still commenting on the photo when Avi returned. Kit looked up at him.

"Everything okay?"

"Not really, but they'll live. Mum was throwing a cosmic hissy fit but I managed to get the occasional word in edgewise. How do you convince mothers that grown men of twenty three can look after themselves and do not need to be baby-sat?"

"Leave home," Kit advised. "It worked for me. Mind you, I had the opposite problem. My mother didn't give a toss where I was just as long as I wasn't interrupting her busy social life." Kit looked sagely at Jo. "Crazies are bad for the family image, you know."

"Anyway," said Jo, "leaving home wouldn't help Avi. It takes more than moving house to shake off our family. They are so possessive. No, Avi doesn't stand a chance. The only son in the household. He's a prized possession. They want him settled down, married off and spawning children - and Aunt Elizabeth is just as bad as Uncle Jacob, even if she started off as a Presbyterian."

Avi shrugged in agreement. "But I'll go down fighting."

"Your denomination sounds horribly like conservative Catholics," said Kelly. "I can empathise, Avrahim. I escaped for precisely the same reasons."

At the same time Jo had been shouting at her father in Beckenham and Kit and Avi had been up-ending boxes of photographs in the Avon Loop, in a tiny flat in Fitzgerald Avenue Cassandra Oakleigh was stepping out of the shower. The stereo was turned up full blast and Cassandra could feel the bass line vibrating the floor boards as she towelled herself dry to the strains of the latest release from 'Charlotte Jane'.

She still thought that 'Charlotte Jane' was a strange name for a rock band, but she knew that it was the name of one of the First Four Ships that brought the early settlers to Christchurch and she had read somewhere that two of the group had degrees from Canterbury University, so she supposed that might account for it. Mind you, neither of them was the one she was interested in. Her friend, Melissa, liked the keyboard player but brown eyes didn't appeal at all to Cassandra. She liked blue eyes. Especially that really striking bright blue like the ones that smouldered down from the posters that engulfed every spare patch of wall space in the microscopic bedsit. Now that man had gorgeous eyes. Cassandra stopped towelling herself and gazed adoringly at one of the posters. Everything about Kester Simmons was gorgeous, she thought. She would make him notice her one day, she had promised herself that.

That was the only reason she had chosen this particular flat. She had looked at others which were larger and sunnier, and some that were cheaper, but this one had the most important factor right - it was only two blocks from Kester's house. Everything else was unimportant.

She had been a fan of 'Charlotte Jane' and, more importantly, of Kester Simmons since the group first hit the music scene in Christchurch six years before. She had been a fan before they had become famous, before being a fan had become the trendy thing to be. She knew more trivia about the band members than any of her friends and she had downloaded every song they had ever put out. She was a real fan. Cassandra had been only twelve years old when she first heard them. They had played at an 'under-age rage' in the Town Hall and she had thought they were just wonderful. She was sure the drummer had smiled right at her and she was determined to catch more than his attention next time. In a moment of brashness Cassandra flung wide her towel to flash her naked body at the poster.

"See what you're missing," she said aloud before turning her back on the picture to don a scanty but exotic set of lacy lingerie in hot pink. She twirled in front of her mirror to survey the effect. Yes! In spite of her limited income, Cassandra had only the best underwear and always made sure she wore a matching set. Brief lace panties, more lace than panty, a brassiere with enough uplift for maximum effect and a filmy camisole designed to look both demure and alluring at the same time. Cassandra would have made a good boy scout; she believed firmly in the adage about being prepared. You never know, today might be the day she got her chance with Kester Simmons and she intended to make very sure that, when the time came, she presented him with an offer he couldn't refuse.

Over the top of the luscious lingerie she added the type of look she imagined appealed to professional rock musicians - stretch denim jeans that clung so tight to her body they appeared to have been applied with a spray can, a halter top that she left partially unbuttoned so the pink lace of the camisole showed invitingly at her up-lifted cleavage, and calf-length, fringed white boots to which she had added silver chains and buckles in imitation of the black boots Kester always appeared in.

She then set about covering her face with an over-heavy

application of make-up; lots of black mascara and eye liner contrasted with emerald green eye shadow and scarlet lipstick. She thought the final effect was mature and sexy, whereas in reality she looked more like a prostitute returning home from a night's work at the local massage parlour, which was a shame as without the make-up Cassandra Oakleigh was a naturally pretty young woman.

From the crowded dressing table beside her bed, Cassandra picked up an ageing silver hair brush and with deft strokes attacked the thick mane of red hair that, if she thought about it, was her most attractive feature. It wasn't a bright, carroty red, but rather a deep, fiery red that reflected different shadings when she moved, and it hung in long, wavy tresses almost to her waist. At the moment, however, the tresses were simply long, damp strands that were dripping water down her neck. She put down her brush and flicked her hair behind her shoulders where it would cause the least amount of discomfort and stooped to pull up the covers on her bed.

This, too, fell under Cassandra's master plan of being prepared. She didn't really need a double bed and she had to admit that it was far too big to fit comfortably in the tiny flat but... maybe one day she and Kester... she thought about that a lot. She knew he had a double bed, she had seen it. She had even touched it, although he didn't know that. She had been to his house several times, but always when he was out.

The first time she had actually hoped he was there. She had been feeling very brave and had marched right up to the front door and wrapped on it with the huge brass lion's head door knocker but it wasn't Kester who had come to the door. It had been a little old lady who had been very nice and had told her that, yes, Kester Simmons did live there but no, he wasn't in at the moment. His grandfather had taken him to his regular doctor's appointment and he was expected back in about an hour. The old lady had offered to let Cassandra come in and wait but her nerve had failed her and she had muttered a quick excuse and left hurriedly.

She hadn't gone near the house again while Kester's grandparents had still been alive but they had died within a month of each other a couple of years ago and since then Kester had lived in the little cottage all by himself. When she found out that piece of news she had made her decision to find a flat close by and make a more determined effort to become indispensable to his lifestyle. It had taken her several months to find just the right place and, in the beginning, she'd been forced to waste an awful amount of time going to work. However, that small inconvenience had been sorted out six months ago - she had been fired. Now she lived on the dole. It may not be as much money as she had earned in that boring office, but it did leave her free to follow what she considered her true vocation - Kester Simmons.

In the last six months she had been to Kester's house several times. Once she had been caught looking in the windows by a neighbour but she had talked her way out of trouble. Then she had discovered a way into the house. The laundry at the back had been a separate structure originally and had old-fashioned louvre windows which were easily removed and replaced. And Kester, bless his heart, only locked the outside door to the porch, not the door that led from the porch into the main body of the house. Since this discovery Cassandra had spent several hours wandering around inside, checking out Kester's possessions. She wasn't very impressed with the collection of memorabilia that had obviously belonged to his grandparents but that wouldn't be a problem, she would enjoy redecorating.

She did like the bed, though. It was one of those big, old, wooden ones with slatted ends; the bed neatly made with a bedspread of homemade patchwork. Cassandra had hunted fruitlessly around several second hand shops before she managed to find one almost like it.

She roughly straightened the covers on her bed then poured herself a cup of strong, black coffee. She didn't like black coffee but she had read that was how Kester drank his, so she had taught herself to, at least, tolerate it. She had drunk it black for so long now she had actually managed to persuade herself that she enjoyed it that way.

Drinking the coffee hurriedly, she turned off the stereo, picked up her mp3 player, attached it to the waistband of her jeans, clamped the headphones to her head, snatched a denim jacket from the debris in the centre of the floor and left the flat for the day.

Cassandra bustled down Fitzgerald Avenue, braving the early morning traffic to reach Cambridge Terrace. From there it was only a short walk to the Barbadoes Street cemetery where she would spend the day. It wasn't that she liked cemeteries, but this particular one gave her a comfortable and sheltered place to sit and an unhindered view of Kester Simmons's house directly opposite on the other side of the river.

Just after she had settled in for her daily vigil, she watched the arrival of the man she couldn't identify. He had been arriving at Kester's every day for the last three weeks, but she didn't know who he was. Logic said he had to be the replacement bass player. The band had not said officially that the old bass player, Gary Ross, had left but it was common gossip. Anyway, the new man carried what was obviously a bass guitar - even an idiot could work that one out. She watched him bike down Oxford Terrace from the Fitzgerald Avenue end and lock his black mountain bike firmly to the inside of Kester's white-painted picket fence.

About a quarter of an hour later, the woman arrived from the direction of the city centre. Cassandra knew who she was. The recent tour publicity had mentioned Joanna Greenwood as a temporary addition to the band's line-up and had given a brief biography which explained that she was an under-graduate of the Christchurch Polytechnic's jazz course, a competent keyboard player in her own right and Avrahim Livingstone's cousin. Cassandra hated her instinctively.

She noticed Livingstone's horrid old car sitting in the driveway. It wasn't like him to be the first to arrive; certainly not before Cassandra herself took up her regular vantage point. Something important must be happening.

After a pause of nearly an hour during which nothing stirred except the ducks on the river, the other two band members arrived in quick succession. Michael Kiesanowski was the first of the pair. He drove up in his snappy, white Honda Accord and parked with precision in front of the house. Daniel Gordon arrived soon after, sliding his green, vintage Valiant Charger to a halt on the wide, grassy riverbank. Even from across the river, Cassandra heard the door slam shut. The legendary temper of the small blond was already up and running. Everybody in the Christchurch music scene had stories of their run-ins with Danny Gordon and his temper, and everyone who told such stories agreed on one thing - he might be small but he was immensely strong and carried a lot of power in his gymnasium-built-up shoulders.

Those inside the house also heard the car door slam. Not a word was said but expressive looks were interchanged. Kit held his breath. The silence that descended as Danny's footsteps approached up the side of the house was finally too much for Jo. By the time Danny attempted to make a dramatic entrance, Jo was writhing on the floor, laughing. Kit was still holding his breath. Avi stretched out a foot and tried to kick Jo into some semblance of cohesion. He failed.

Danny posed in the doorway. He glared at his fellow musicians, snorted under his breath, turned and strutted out to the workshop. The others eyed each other with amusement. Kit breathed.

CHAPTER SIX

Mike Kiesanowski was first to his feet.

"Come on, you guys. We may as well get this rehearsal under way. Can't say I'm looking forward to it much, though. Oh, by the way," he lowered his voice conspiratorially, "I asked Sarah if she could 'accidentally' call in at lunch time. She's going to try and get Danny aside and have a quiet word with him."

"Good idea," agreed Avi, also hauling himself to his feet. "Sarah, Mike's wife, is a psychologist," he explained to Kelly and Jo who were looking puzzled at the reference. "She's a seriously useful person to talk to if you ever have any problems you can't work out by yourself."

He grinned meaningfully at Kit and offered a hand to help Kit up. Kit took the offer and smiled back.

"Yeah, she is, but so are you." He turned to the others. "Avi's just being modest. He's got a fancy degree in psychology as well, he just doesn't tell people about it."

Avi shrugged. "It's not relevant to what I'm doing at the moment. Yeah, Sarah and I did our degrees together. She chose to use hers, I didn't. My other degree in music is more important to me."

"It must have been interesting, though?" queried Kelly.

"Oh yeah, granted. And granted it can be very useful at times. I just don't see myself as a professional in the field, like Sarah. That wasn't why I did it."

"Why did you do it?"

"Personal reasons." Avi grinned again at Kit.

"Fair enough."

"Come on!" Mike stirred them up again. "Let's get on with it."

Jo and Kelly pushed aside the pile of photographs and stood up, Jo swinging an upraised arm forwards in the motion used by cavalry officers in western movies to denote the command for "Charge!"

"Yo!" she said with false enthusiasm. "Forward Ho! Into the fray!"

Avi placed his hand on the small of Kit's back.

"Come on," he said gently. "Let's get this over and done with."

Kit returned the gesture by placing his own arm over Avi's narrow shoulders.

"Yeah, I guess so."

Mike, Kelly and Jo misunderstood the exchange completely.

Out in the workshop, Danny was already plugging the labyrinth of cable leads into assorted amplifiers. Kelly and Mike unpacked their guitars and grabbed a lead each, both running off a few quick riffs to check the sound levels. Jo grabbed a microphone from a stand and chattered nonsense into it to make sure it, too, was live. It wasn't but Danny soon remedied the situation, finding the relevant piece of cable and slotting it into its correct input socket. Avi was quickly head down over his keyboard, checking all its assorted buttons and keys. Kit slid in behind his drums, adjusted the tension of the black-shelled maple snare, grabbed a set of sticks from the bag behind him on the floor and ran a series of smooth rolls quickly over the toms. Danny paused in his work, impressed.

"Welcome back, Mr Simmons. You're on the ball again

today."

Kit decided to be polite.

"Yeah, sorry about the last couple of days. I had a bit of a problem but it's under control now."

"It had better be." Danny's snarled reply showed he wasn't giving that much quarter. "Can we get under way?"

"Actually, no." Avi looked up from his keyboard. "Kit and I have something to tell you all before we start rehearsing."

"Oh, for God's sake!" The tenuous hold Danny had over his hot temper dissipated. "Livingstone, I don't want to hear if you and Simmons are finally announcing your engagement! I don't even care if Simmons is pregnant! Your earth-shattering revelations can wait until after this goddamned rehearsal!"

Avi smiled thinly. "No, they can't, actually. It happens to be pretty important and you'd better listen, Danny, because it probably effects the whole band and might just effect the tour."

Avi paused for effect. Nobody spoke, not even Danny. Avi continued, explaining about the crank calls.

"...and if Kit isn't crazy, and things are going missing inside his house, we have to assume... well, I'm damned if I know what to assume," he finished.

"Maybe that's just lack of sleep." Danny was interested now.

"I don't follow," said Kit.

"Well, you know, maybe you were so tired you weren't thinking straight and just couldn't remember where you put things. A bit like being drunk, you think you know exactly what you're doing when you do it, it just doesn't make sense later when you sober up."

"Probably," Kit conceded. "You could be right."

"So," Danny took control. "Are you reporting this to the police? If so, have you done so already or do we leave it until after the tour and just keep our tour security extra tight?"

"That's why we wanted to talk to you guys," said Avi. "I'm all for telling the police today. After all, it's going to be a bit difficult, not to mention stressful, coping with all the hassles of a tour on top of the knowledge that there's some kind of loony trailing around after us... well, after Kit, to be more precise." He looked up at Kit who was leaning forward on his drums. "Sorry, Kit, I don't mean to embarrass you in public but, let's face it, out of all of us, you are the worst one that could have been targeted. Kit was freaking out in a big way yesterday. If this carries on right through the tour, he's never going to handle it, are you, Kit?"

"Well..." Kit didn't sound convinced.

"Not to mention," Avi continued, "Kit's going to be leaving his house unattended. I think the police should be told now so they can keep an eye on it."

"I think you're right," Mike agreed. "I vote we rehearse now and call the police during the lunch break."

"Good idea." Danny clapped his hands to stimulate them into action. "Let's try 'Toleration' from the top, in A."

Jo leaned forwards and whispered in Mike's ear.

"I'd like to see 'Toleration' in D, for Danny."

Mike laughed.

For the next couple of hours the rehearsal flowed smoothly. Kit was relaxed after a decent night's sleep and his drumming showed the return of his usual touch of genius. Danny turned his aggression into his music and churned through song after song with a hard metal edge that left Mike and Avi grinning and nodding with pleasure. By the time he signalled a lunch break, even Danny was smiling.

"Ace!" He offered high praise. "That, you guys, was ace! Hey," he turned to Avi but gestured towards Kit, "Give your funny mate there a cigarette, he's earned one for a change."

Avi pulled the ever-present packet of Rothmans from his pocket and gestured it invitingly towards Kit who nodded his interest as he stepped away from his drums, stretching his body to remove the kinks in his muscles. Avi produced a cigarette lighter.

"Not in here, you don't!" Jo admonished him sharply.

Avi shrugged. Jo had placed a no-smoking ban inside the workshop on her first day with the group. In spite of it being Kit's property, the two smokers had been quickly out-voted. Danny and Kelly, both health food and fitness fanatics, agreed with Jo's arguments about smoke versus singing ability and about their right not to have to smoke second-hand and Mike staunchly refused to take sides. Avi had attempted to maintain their previous status quo but Kit had turned out to be something of a turn-coat, siding with the non-smokers on the grounds that their arguments made sense, he couldn't drum and smoke at the same time and that he didn't mind an excuse to go outside anyway. He did firmly maintain, however, that the ban applied only to the workshop and that inside his own house he would do exactly as he liked. That statement had surprised Avi; Kit wasn't normally so assertive.

"All right! All right!" Avi sniped back at Jo. "Give us a chance! Hmm! You get more like your mother every day, and, trust me, that isn't a compliment!"

Avi stalked determinedly out of the workshop straight

into the path of Sarah Kiesanowski who was coming in, carrying a large tapestry-covered handbag, a baby and a packed lunch.

"Avi, darling!" she said effusively as he stepped back to let her enter. "Here, take Rosie for me." Without giving him time to think, Sarah thrust the baby into his arms. The chubby-faced, frilly-clad creature stared up at Avi and gurgled meaninglessly.

Sarah Kiesanowski was a small, bird-like woman who filled a room more by her personality than by her size. She overflowed with boundless energy, of which she always seemed to have plenty to spare, even after juggling a full professional life with three girls under the age of five. In her full calf-length skirt and matching blouse in vibrant yellow, her entrance exploded an air of summer into the otherwise sombre-hued workshop.

Mike put down his guitar and rushed to embrace his wife before relieving Avi of his unbidden burden. Avi heaved a sigh of relief. It wasn't that he didn't like, or wasn't used to, holding Sarah and Mike's offspring, he just never felt quite at ease doing so, unlike Kit who thought the three little girls were simply wonderful and would happily baby-sit them whenever he was asked. Sarah put down her bag and her lunch and turned back to have another look at Avi. She ran the back of her fingers over the still-unshaven stubble on his face.

"What's this, Avi? You're not growing a beard, surely?"

Avi sniggered. "No. I just didn't shave last night."

"Don't let it become a habit. It doesn't become you."

"No, ma'am."

She kissed him lightly on the cheek.

"It's good to see you, even if you do look awful. You haven't been to visit me for ages."

"Sorry, I've been flat out trying to get some grade four and five pupils through their piano exams before I take off on tour."

"Well you have to come to dinner before you leave." She walked over to Kit who was making gooing noises at the baby. "And you," she ordered, kissing him as well, "Chelsea will be furious if you go on tour without saying goodbye. She keeps asking when 'Uncle Kethter ith going to wead her another thtowy'." She imitated the voice of a small child.

Kit laughed, blushing slightly.

"Yeah, all right. But I'm just about out of stories. I think Chelsea can read better than I can now."

Sarah laughed back, putting out a hand to move Kit's unruly hair from in front of his face. She put her head on one side and studied him for a moment. Kit dropped his gaze and blushed again.

"You look relaxed today. That's good," she said.

"Yeah, I'm okay," Kit agreed. He didn't want to rehash the previous day again.

"Good," Sarah repeated. She wanted to know more but wasn't going to ask. Mike had told her about the tensions that had overflowed into violence and, from past experience, she had expected to find Kit in a state of stress. She correctly assumed the reason he wasn't was due to Avi. Still exuding cheerful good humour, Sarah turned her attention to Danny.

"Daniel," she said, putting a hand on each of his tightly muscle-bound upper arms and holding him back at arm's length, "my, don't you look good. You must be putting in hours at the gym."

She let him go with a sweet smile, knowing full well that if there was one thing Danny Gordon couldn't resist, it was a woman stroking his super-macho ego. As she had expected he drew himself up to his full five foot four inches of height and, almost subconsciously, flexed his chest and arms. Knowing she was being naughty and knowing, too, that Mike would tease her about it afterwards, Sarah batted her eyelashes and continued the fulsome praise.

"It was your name I saw in the paper the other day, wasn't it?" she asked. "In the article on the power lifting competition? What was it again, second in your class?"

"In two of my events, yeah," Danny replied, pride swelling his chest even further. "I've got another competition coming up in twelve week's time. That means I'm going to have to watch myself when we're touring and work really hard when we get back, but I'm pretty confident I can win this time. The chap who beat me last time is good, sure, but I reckon I'm better than him and I intend to prove it."

Sarah looked suitably impressed.

"You must work very hard on your body to be that strong. How many hours do you spend in the gym each day?"

"At least four." Danny was always willing to talk about body building. Making music was a great way to get fame and adulation but it was always full of setbacks and frustrations. Body building was beautiful. It was his passion. Sure there was pain but the gain was visible, you could see it in the mirror, you could feel it when you moved. It got you respect. Nobody hassled Danny Gordon about being short, not more than once anyway. Yeah, granted Kiesanowski had knocked him to the ground yesterday but, fair's fair, he had taken him by surprise and Kiesanowski was no wimp. "It varies," he continued, "depending on whether there's a competition coming up and what we're doing with the band, but four's a good average."

"Average!" Sarah laughed, a rippling, birdlike trill. "That would be an average yearly workout for me, not a daily one."

"That's all right." Danny wasn't intentionally condescending, his attitude was an unfortunate natural tendency. "I wouldn't expect you'd be able to lift any of the weights anyway. After all, you're only a woman."

Danny was not aware of the supreme effort Sarah put into maintaining her smile and not kicking her delicate, feminine toes firmly into his masculinity. However, while Danny was unaware of Sarah's indelicate thoughts, Mike knew his wife only too well. He correctly discerned it to be a good time to steer the conversation in another direction. Quickly.

"Sarah, love," he moved forwards and held out the baby. "I think Rosie wants you."

Sarah's attention turned instinctively to her daughter and the tension eased noticeably.

"Shall we eat lunch?" Mike's smile at the sight of his wife and youngest child was unaffected. Sarah had picked him up unashamedly six years before when the band, then young and still trashy, had played a lunch-time gig at the University of Canterbury's amphitheatre. Mike was then in his second year of a Masters addition to his degree in engineering. He had been both surprised and flattered when Avi had approached him in a break between sets to inform him that a friend of his from his psychology class 'wanted his body, no questions asked'. He was even more surprised when he realised that the girl who had sent Avi on the mission was absolutely gorgeous. Mike had gone willingly and had been her besotted and devoted slave ever since. He wasn't sure what she saw in him but he wasn't complaining.

"Of course, darling," Sarah turned her dazzling smile on her husband. "I grabbed a little something as I passed the french bakery. It's in the bag." She gestured vaguely towards the tapestry handbag which now lay propped up against an amplifier.

"Great! I'm starving." Mike headed for the bag. "Danny's been working us like dogs."

"No worse than you can expect on tour." Danny's tone was grudging. He couldn't prove it, but he felt there was an underlying tone in Mike's remark which was meant as a personal slight. Danny was an expert in taking offence.

"Hey!" Kit favoured Avi with his best pathetic under-dog look. "If you're not going to give me that cigarette, can you at least get out of the bloody doorway so I can go and get my own?"

Avi again held out the cigarettes invitingly but jumped nimbly out the door as Kit reached for the packet. Laughing, Kit followed him out and quickly made use of his vastly superior height and arm length to overpower his friend and wrestle the offending article from him. Avi succumbed with little prompting and voluntarily handed over the necessary lighter. Kit lit a cigarette and handed both packet and lighter back to Avi with a gracious "thank you". Avi, still panting slightly from the exertion, lit one for himself.

"What are we doing for food?" he asked.

Kit shrugged.

"The usual?" Avi suggested. "Hot bread shop?"

Kit threw Avi a look that suggested it might be a good idea but hadn't Avi forgotten that Kit had no money. Avi responded by giving Kit a hearty slap on the back.

"Mellow out, Kester! It's my suggestion, I'll pay."

"I can't keep doing this. I can't owe you this much. I can't pay you back." Kit's voice was beginning to sound strained.

"Then just accept it. I told you yesterday, I don't want it paid back. Look, you demolished lunch yesterday in five seconds flat. You were obviously starving. And you made pretty short work of dinner. You had nothing at all in your kitchen, and I mean nothing, not even a slice of bread. How many days had you gone without any food? How many?"

"Um... that was the second." Kit ducked his head and shrugged his shoulders in combined move of gawky embarrassment.

"Oh!" Avi sighed his frustration. "I wish you'd come to me with your problems. Look, forget the money for now. We eat lunch, I pay, no problems, no questions. Later on, this evening, after we've sorted this other mess out with the police and we've finished rehearsing, we'll sit down together and take a look at your finances. Okay? I'm sure we can sort something out."

"But Mum and Gabriel do all that. I wouldn't know where to start."

"Oh, come on, Kit! You're not that stupid! It's simple maths, you were better than me at maths at school. Come on, let's get lunch."

Kit let himself be led away, unresisting.

"Wait up, you two!" Jo's voice shouted. Kit and Avi turned to see Jo and Kelly sprinting after them. "Wait up!"

"Hot bread shop?" inquired Avi needlessly of Jo.

"You betcha!"

"And you, Kelly? Peace, love and mung beans as usual?"

"Of course. I would do else?" Kelly replied, tossing his spiky-cropped head haughtily in mock offence.

"What about the others?"

"Nah!" Jo answered. "Sarah's brought this obscene-looking french loaf for her and Mike and Danny's got his own with him, some horrid looking instant-muscles-in-a-sachet-just-add-water junk. Yuk!"

"It's undoubtedly a lot healthier than all that cream and pastry you inflict on your poor body," Kelly lectured.

"Shut up! Who asked you anyway?" Jo gave no quarter.

"Avrahim?" Kelly inquired, determined not to let Jo have the last say. "You eat by some sort of strict religious guidelines, don't you?"

"Yeah, sort of."

"And I am right in believing that Joanna here is your cousin?"

"Yeah." Avi began to see where Kelly was leading.

"So Joanna is bound by the same rules?"

"Sorry, Kelly, you can't run any further down that track. The rules I grew up with are how my father reads the Bible, not how anybody else does. I may seem to be more staunch than Jo but that's because my father is way more scary than hers. Every time I look at something I know my father wouldn't approve of, I can imagine him preaching at me. Kind of stops me in my tracks, even now. Anyway, I don't particularly like cream cakes."

"Oh, ok. I must admit I did wonder if you two were Jewish and you kept kosher, I was just too polite to ask."

"It might be easier if we were. At least the crazy rules would have some historical sense instead of just being the weird ramblings of some hippy."

"What?"

"Back in the early 70s. Some hippy dude who had been thrown out of some Hutterite community in America, discovered the good life in San Francisco then swung back the other way again and became a holy-roller born-again preacher with the worst vision of hell and damnation you've ever heard. Came out here and started a commune, wrote his own rules. My dad and Jo's mum were early converts. They were still only teenagers. They even changed their names to something biblical – Dad went from Mark to Jacob and Jo's Mum, Miriam, used to be Sandra. Jo's parents have mellowed a bit over the years but Dad gets stricter as he gets older. Say, Kit, isn't that your mother?"

Kit's gaze followed in the direction Avi pointed. Down a tiny side street his mother and three men stood clustered outside one of the neatly maintained cottages. One of the men was holding a real estate agent's 'For Sale' sign.

"Yeah." Kit put his head down and hurried on.

"Aren't you going to speak?"

"No."

"You could hit her up for some money."

"In front of her workmates? You've got to be joking. I'd never hear the end of it."

They hurried on their way to the shops, Kelly diverging as expected to the health food shop on the opposite side of the road.

"Good morning, afternoon, whatever." The owner greeted them like an old friends. "Cream donut is it, Jo?"

"And an eclair. He's paying." She pointed to Avi.

"Kester?" He knew them all by name. He was very proud of that. He liked to make it known to as many people as would listen that he knew the members of 'Charlotte Jane' by name.

"Um... a mince pie, please. Um... and a cheese roll... if that's okay?" The question was directed at Avi.

"Sure." Avi nodded. "My shout," he explained to the shopkeeper. "Make that two pies and two cheese rolls, I'll have the same as Kit," he added.

"Sure thing. Mike not with you today?" Danny never ate with the rest of the group and Kelly shopped elsewhere.

"He's back at the workshop. His wife and kid are visiting, brought lunch with them."

"Tell him I said hello."

"Yeah, sure." Avi handed over a twenty dollar note and collected the change.

As Avi pocketed his money and chatted with the shopkeeper, Kit turned to leave, crashing as he did so into a young woman who was just entering the shop.

"Sorry," said Kit quickly, putting out a hand instinctively to steady her.

Cassandra Oakleigh looked up into her hero's concerned and embarrassed face. At such close quarters, barely two inches from his chest, she was suddenly aware just how very tall he was. She noticed, too, that his skin was pale. No healthy New Zealand tan. On the contrary, his skin was almost translucent, the encroaching five o'clock shadow of facial hair, even though it was only lunch time and even though Kit had shaved as usual that morning, adding a blue tinge. Or was that just a reflection from his eyes. They really were as vivid as the colours on the poster in her bedroom. Sometimes she had looked at the poster and thought the colours must have been enhanced. Nobody had eyes that blue. But he did, he really did.

Cassandra tentatively, very tentatively, reached out a hand to touch Kit's bare arm. She noticed that his arms, too, were covered in a downy coating of jet black hair.

"Sorry," Kit said again. "Are you okay?"

His voice was so deep. She hadn't imagined that. She hadn't heard him speak before. He didn't do interviews, they were left to Danny Gordon, who sang the songs, and Avi Livingstone, who seemed to be the 'power behind the throne'. Kester Simmons didn't like talking to people. But he had just spoken to her. Okay? She felt weak at the knees and sick to her stomach but she had never felt better.

"Yeah, yeah, I'm fine." She found her voice and smiled up into those blue, blue eyes that flashed into brilliance as a matching smile - in reality of relief, but Cassandra was happy to misconstrue it as pleasure in her company - lifted Kit's concerned expression.

Kit, who was feeling profoundly embarrassed and shy at having crashed into a complete stranger, quickly dropped his hand from her shoulder and attempted to step back out of her way. However, the young woman moved with him, maintaining their close body contact and her hold on his arm. She inclined her head slightly to include the others.

"You're 'Charlotte Jane', aren't you?" She posed coquettishly.

"Yeah." It was Avi who replied.

"And you," smiling enticingly up at Kit, she ran her index finger suggestively up and down the wiry, hardened muscle of his upper arm, "you're Kester Simmons." A statement phrased as a question.

"I guess," Kit shrugged. He felt decidedly uncomfortable.

"I'm Cassandra," she said, still over-acting the seductress role. "I live near you. I've got all your cds."

"Um..." Kit was floundering.

"You'll be coming to our concert, then." Avi stepped in.

"Oh, yes. I'll be right up the front, as always."

"I don't mean to intrude but are you three coming or are you setting up camp in here?" Kelly's arrival couldn't have been better timed.

"Just coming." Avi jumped at the interruption, pushed himself between Kit and the girl and propelled Kit out the door. "Bye, See you later," he called back into the shop.

"Yep, that's 'Charlotte Jane', all right," Jo heard the shopkeeper tell the girl as the musicians departed. "They buy their lunch here all the time when they're rehearsing. They're good friends of mine."

Cassandra, on the other hand, heard only Kit's murmured words to Avi as the door closed behind them.

"Neat coloured hair!"

CHAPTER SEVEN

"Are you worried about the tour?"

Mike had taken the baby from the workshop into the cottage on the pretext of cleaning the pair of them up before lunch, but really so Sarah could talk to Danny uninterrupted.

"No," Danny snapped an angry reply. "Why should I be worried? We've got a brand new bass player who's still learning half the songs, a backing singer who stuffs cream cakes down her throat faster than Heidi the Hippopotamus in the 'Meet the Feebles' movie and who never knows when to shut up, and that's just her good side, and a faggot of a drummer who's so tanked up on junk he can't string a complete sentence together... and ten days left! Why should I be worried?"

"Indeed," Sarah said in her calm, level, professional voice. "Why should you worry? Danny, think about it another way, none of those things are your responsibility, they're not your problem."

"Don't be ridiculous? How can you say that?"

"It's obvious," Sarah shrugged. "Let's look at this a different way."

"How?"

"Well, to begin with, don't treat it as one huge overwhelming problem. Let's break it down and take a look at the constituent bits, shall we?"

"Okay." Danny's agreement was grudging.

"Fine. Let's start with Kelly. How many songs does he still have to learn?"

"Oh," Danny gave in with a heavy sigh. "None, I guess."

He flung his arms wide in a gesture of hopelessness. "He knows them all basically, he just does some of the riffs differently. He's just... he's just not Gary!"

"So you would have to admit, honestly, that Kelly isn't really a problem at all. Musically he knows what he's doing, it's just that you preferred working with Gary. Right?"

"Yeah." Danny mumbled his assent.

"So, you see," Sarah continued cheerfully, "that's one problem solved already. Easy, isn't it? Now, what's next? Jo."

"I don't like her. She's like Livingstone, just because she's getting some fancy music letters after her name she thinks she's God's little gift to us all. I didn't want her in the group. I don't think we need her at all."

"But the others do."

"Huh!"

"Isn't the purpose of this tour to publicise the new album?"

"So?"

"Well, Jo did sing the backing on the album and she did co-write a couple of the songs. The songs wouldn't sound the same if you left the backing out now."

"Hmmm!" Danny wasn't going to admit defeat again. "I suppose you're going to stick up for Simmons as well?"

Sarah laughed lightly.

"I don't think I have to, Danny. You know as well as I do that Kit comes with the territory. He's a founder member of the group. You're wrong about him still being on drugs. He's worked extremely hard to get his act cleaned up and he's doing very well. It really doesn't matter whether you agree or disagree with his lifestyle, if your only concern is with the way the band sounds when it's on stage then you've got no worries in regards to Kit - even in the days when he was using heavily he never missed a performance and he never missed a beat. Kit may be a lot of things you don't approve of, but he's first and foremost a professional musician."

"Musician? Garbage!" Danny spat. "He's not a musician, he's only a drummer!"

"You ignorant bastard!" The shouted counter-attack came from Mike, who had entered unseen and placed his baby daughter quietly on the floor. Now he strode over to come between his wife and Danny. Danny took a step back, bracing himself for another physical attack but Mike's anger was cold, his voice quiet and, somehow, more deadly because of that.

"I'm sick of you, Gordon. I've had you, right up to here," Mike indicated the top of his head. "I dare you, say that again, to Kit, face to face, you gutless little prick!"

"Easy." Sarah wormed her way between them. "That's enough. Michael, don't leave Rosie on the floor, she'll get dirty. Danny, just calm down and think about what I said. Don't take on problems that aren't yours. Your only responsibility is to get up there every night, play your guitar and sing the songs. You've got four other competent musicians who all know what they're doing, and it's their responsibility if they don't, a road crew to worry about the gear and a manager to worry about anything else. Take it easy."

Danny walked away without saying a word. They heard his heavy stride retreat down the gravel driveway and a few moments later a strident roar as his V8 car thundered into life.

"You're right," Sarah nodded to Mike. "He's a bit tetchy,

isn't he?”

"A bit tetchy? Is that your professional description? Downright, bloodymindedly pig-ignorant, I would say." Mike was still seething but that didn't stop him ripping a large chunk off the bread roll from the bag and stuffing it into his mouth.

"Well," Sarah giggled at Mike's reaction. "I daresay tetchy isn't a very professional term. He is certainly very strung out and if he was a client of mine I would have grave doubts as to the veracity of his story. Somehow I think there is something bothering him a lot more than just Kelly's playing, Jo's cream cakes or Kester's sex life."

"He has one?"

"One what? Who?"

"Kit. A sex life. I didn't think he had one."

"Oh, Michael! Honestly! Eat your lunch."

Danny hadn't really intended to leave, he didn't have anywhere to go, but his pent-up fury had to be directed into some kind of action and driving the huge car seemed the only obvious choice. It was a choice he took frequently when he was too angry to do anything else. He drove as far as the brewery on Kilmore Street, about half a city block, bought himself a rigger of their special beer, then drove back to Kit's house, squealing the tyres satisfyingly when he pulled up. He knew he was in training and shouldn't be drinking the beer but at that moment he didn't care. A beer would be good. As he left and locked his car he saw the other four band members walking towards the house from the other direction. He didn't wait for them, but stalked up the drive and into the workshop, pointedly ignoring the Kiesanowskis who were laughing together over a private joke. Danny would have bet money that he was the subject. He would have lost.

The others, too, were laughing when they re-entered. Well, three were laughing while Kit twitched uncomfortably.

"You'll never guess," Jo couldn't keep the news to herself, "Kit has an admirer."

"Leave it out, Jo" pleaded Kit. He dissociated himself from the others and sloped over to the electric jug to make himself a mug of coffee.

The plea had no effect. Jo launched into a spirited impression of Cassandra, using Kelly as a substitute Kit.

"Oh, you must be Kester Simmons," she over-acted in an atrociously fake Southern American accent, rubbing her body salaciously over Kelly who was grinning broadly and offering no objections. "Oh, I have aaall your cds." Jo drawled the vowel into three syllables.

"Leave it out, Jo!" Kit snapped angrily this time. There was an edge to his tone which Avi picked up as a warning sign but Jo failed to notice.

"What are you lot talking about?" Mike queried from around a piece of french loaf.

Jo, still bouncing, extricated herself from around Kelly's unresisting body and happily explained.

"There was this bimbo down at the bakery. Skin tight clothes, flame red hair and make-up done with a palette knife. Kit, the clumsy oaf, just about knocked her over and the next thing we know she's all over him like a rash. Personally, I thought she was going to rape him over the coffee buns." Jo wasn't about to let the truth spoil a good story.

"It wasn't really that bad." Avi corrected quietly. "A fan of ours, it seems, who obviously lives near here. Although I must say Jo is right on one aspect - she did seem to prefer Kit to anyone else."

"That's only because she hadn't met me," Kelly smirked. "It would seem that there is only one other relevant question, then - was the attraction mutual, Kester?"

Sarah glanced at Avi and stifled a giggle.

"Um... well... not really... um," Kit stammered, blushing. "Not... um... my type."

"So what is your type then?" Jo was curious.

"I would have thought that was common knowledge," Danny sneered. "Simmons likes pretty piano boys wrapped in denim." Danny looked pointedly at Avi who glared stonily back. "And," Danny continued, "sprinkled lightly with heroin."

Kit responded without warning. The half-full mug of coffee was propelled with all the force he could muster. It travelled in a straight trajectory half the distance of the workshop before meeting its intended target - Danny's forehead. For the second time in three days Daniel Gordon slumped to the ground in a trickle of his own blood. For a split second nobody reacted, then everybody reacted at once. Kit cut and ran, slamming the door shut after him. Avi followed Kit, far more concerned with his friend than with his guitarist, who had deserved all he got. Sarah picked up the baby. Kelly and Jo backed away.

"I think I put my foot in my mouth again," Jo said quietly.

"I think we all did," Kelly replied.

"Danny sure as hell did."

"Somewhat."

Out of the entire group, Mike was the only one who bothered to attend to Danny. Not that he knew what to do. Still, that didn't stop him going through the motions. He knelt beside Danny, pulled an immaculately laundered handkerchief from the pocket of his camel coloured slacks and futilely dabbed at the conglomeration of blood and coffee that ran down Danny's face and soaked into the front of his erstwhile white t-shirt. Sarah approached, holding out a second handkerchief which she had wet in the tiny sink. Mike took it and cleaned around the cut which, once cleared of the smeared debris, turned out to be long but shallow. Mike folded his own handkerchief into a pad which he held against the cut, relinquishing his hold to Danny as the smaller man began to stir. Danny rose unsteadily to his feet, supported by Mike, and fell into an armchair, breathing heavily. For a while he sat back, handkerchief pressed against his forehead, moaning softly, but as Avi re-entered, leading a subdued Kit, Danny's volatile temper overrode any pain he was feeling. He leapt to his feet, strode over to Kit and, as Mike had done to him two days before, slammed Kit backwards into the wall.

"You're fired, Simmons! As of right now! I don't want you anywhere near me! You're fired! Understand? Fired!"

Avi stepped between them.

"Sit down, Danny." His tone was quiet but brooked no disagreement.

Danny glared but Avi matched his gaze, forcing Danny to back off. He slouched back to the armchair and resumed the position of injured martyr.

"I meant what I said," he repeated. "I'm not working with Simmons again. He's not a gentle little depressive, he's a psychopath! A violent, unpredictable psychopath!"

"Look who's talking," Jo muttered in a quiet aside to Kelly. They were both still holed up a safe distance from any possible line of fire - behind the rack of amplifiers.

"One difference," Kelly replied pedantically. "Daniel is violent but he is not, you would agree, unpredictable. Rather, his violence is somewhat par for the course."

"Sad, but true," Jo agreed.

"I mean it!" Danny was still in full flight. "The bastard's fired!"

"No he isn't." Avi was adamant.

"Yes he bloody well is."

"The decision isn't yours to make," Avi stated categorically.

"Avi's right." Mike stepped forwards. "You may be the frontman, Danny, but you don't make the decisions. Musically, sure, you pretty much get it your own way but only because you're the one doing the vocals, but business decisions - no way, mate - you get your opinion listened to, you may even get a vote, but if you think you get any say in who goes and who stays, read that precious contract of yours again, mate."

Mike had now moved from beside Danny's chair to stand in front of it, shoulder to shoulder with Avi who continued the explanation.

"In your contract's small print you will find that 'Charlotte Jane' is a legal entity consisting of myself, Mike here, Pete Branston, now resident in Australia but still receiving his cut, and," he paused for dramatic effect, "Kester Simmons." Avi bestowed on Danny a beatific smile. "You can't fire Kit, Danny, he's your boss."

Jo nudged Kelly and unsuccessfully stifled a giggle. Jo always loved a show-down and she was thoroughly enjoying this one.

"Isn't Avi wonderful when he's being masterful," she whispered sarcastically. "He's normally so busy being deferential and polite I thought he was a mousy little wimp."

"That is not a nice way to consider your relatives," Kelly admonished.

"Maybe not but, come on now, it's fairly accurate."

Kelly answered with a non-committal shrug.

Danny eyed Avi, Mike and Kit in icy silence. Kit, surprisingly, made the first move to break the deadlock.

"I'm sorry, Danny." He looked genuinely contrite and even Jo and Kelly, from the other side of the room, could see he was shaking. "Look... um...," he wrung his hands in distraction. "I know you must all be pretty pissed off with me at the moment... um... I know I'm messing things up real bad. I'm really sorry." Kit's breath was erratic and it was obvious he was fighting to hold back his distress. "Look... um... I promise I won't make any more trouble. Honestly, Danny, I'll stay out of your way, I promise. I don't want to ruin the tour."

"No, you're damn right you won't ruin the tour. I won't let you," Danny said after a long moment's contemplation. "All right, since it looks like I have no choice, let's agree on one thing. I don't want to see you, I don't want to hear you. You just keep your nose clean, shut up and play the drums. And, by God, you'd better do that well or, boss or no boss, you won't see the end of the tour."

Kit didn't argue. His whole body was reacting to the shock of what he had done. Nauseous and shaking uncontrollably, he took refuge where he knew he was on safe ground - behind his drums; the visually impressive array of black-lacquered maple and shining metal creating an effective fortress wall between him and the rest of the world.

"Come on!" Danny ordered. He dabbed at the wound on his head for a final time then thrust the coffee and blood soaked handkerchief back into Mike's unresponsive hand. "Let's get back to work!"

Sarah, clutching her baby tightly, grabbed for both her bag and her husband.

"I think I'll leave," she whispered in Mike's ear. "Good luck. Avi," she pulled her friend aside. "Can you manage Kit?"

"Yeah," Avi nodded.

"Call me if you need me. Any time."

"Yeah. Thanks. Sorry you got caught in the middle of that."

"Don't worry." She patted him reassuringly on the arm. "I see worse at the office. Bye." Sarah slipped away.

Avi, like the others, took up his stage position although the atmosphere was unnaturally quiet. Danny gave the order for the song and the count down, Kit and Kelly opened with a rhythm section introduction and the day's rehearsal restarted. For an hour the rehearsal ran remarkably smoothly, considering the studied calm under which everyone was performing. However, just when the icy atmosphere began to thaw, Mike's amplifier screeched into feedback and exploded in a puff of black smoke.

"Hell!" Mike jumped involuntarily then hurriedly began unplugging his guitar and flicking off power switches.

Danny, muttering oaths under his breath, propped his

own guitar on its stand and hurried over. He whipped a Swiss Army knife from his pocket and in a few minutes had the amplifier apart and the damaged part identified.

"You're lucky. It's not a serious problem," he said to a relieved Mike. "Here, take a look."

Mike took his turn peering into the amplifier's insides then pronounced his judgment.

"You're right. Can we fix it now?"

"Now? No. I don't have the part. But, what the hell, it's been a bitch of a day anyway. Let's call it quits. I'll go into town and get what I need and come back later and fix the thing. She'll be right by tomorrow."

Mike had to concede that Danny knew what he was doing. He had paid his dues as a roadie and could be relied on to fix any piece of equipment that broke down. Even if he was a creep!

"Okay!" Mike straightened up to face the others. "That's it. She's history for the day. Wind it up!"

His announcement was greeted with sighs of gratitude.

"Yeah, forget it, you guys," Danny agreed. "We can't do any more till I've fixed this heap of shit." He kicked the amplifier.

"Hey!" Mike expostulated. "That heap of shit happens to be mine!"

"You want to fix it then?" Danny retorted petulantly.

"Doesn't bother me." Mike called his bluff.

"Huh!"

Mike's calling of the bluff was correct. Danny wasn't about to give up even the smallest chance to look important. The little man took another hurried look inside the workings of the amplifier then made ready to leave. However, unable to resist having the final say, he turned in the doorway.

"Today was okay but I want some real action out of you lot again tomorrow. Time is running out. Reynolds, I'm still not happy with that riff in 'Pieces'. I don't care what your arguments are, I want it back the way Gary played it. Pronto!"

Kelly shrugged in resignation but said nothing.

"Livingstone!" Danny continued. "A word of warning. In advance. Tomorrow might be Friday but I don't give a damn about your religious sensibilities right now. We're rehearsing late tomorrow, and I mean well into the evening, and we'll be rehearsing all day Saturday, whether you like it or not! That goes for you, too, Greenwood."

"Hey, don't lump me with him!" Jo protested. "I don't give a stuff. Just 'cos he's super-conservative, doesn't mean we all are. I gave it up for pizzas."

"Good." Danny's tone dripped with sarcasm. "Then we can expect your full attention on the music, can't we? Simmons." He swept Kit, who was still cowering behind his drums, with a look of disgust. "No, to hell with you! I don't want to talk to you, you're scum!"

Having delivered what he considered to be a suitably impressive exit line, Danny exited. Only then was Kit game enough to come out of his self-imposed exile. He checked his watch.

"Hey, do you guys want to come into the house for a coffee, or something, before you go?"

There was a general murmuring and shrugging of shoulders before Jo answered.

"Yeah, why not? I want another look at those ridiculous photos. Lead the way."

Again there was generalised movement as each musician unplugged and packed away their instruments. Mike looked at Danny's Gibson, still resting on its stand.

"Should I pack it up, or kick it to death?" He laughed maliciously.

"Turn off the amp and leave it where it is," Avi advised, although his tone was cold. "It's his bloody problem."

"Yeah," Kit agreed. "Whatever we do with it will be wrong, so leave the stuffing thing where it is."

"Oh!" Mike sounded as if he had hoped they would back his request to damage the instrument, although his grin belied his tone. "Yeah, I guess we can't blame the guitar for the faults of its owner."

"Which are many," concluded Avi.

"Only one, I would have thought," interposed Kit.

"Only one?" Avi queried.

"Yeah. He breathes."

Instruments safely packed away, the five band members left the workshop, pausing in the garden while Kit turned the giant key which locked the heavy tongue-in-groove door, and filed into the cottage where they strewed themselves over various pieces of furniture. Kit remained in the kitchen, making coffee. His inputs into the conversation seemed chirpy enough although nobody failed to notice, as he delivered the coffee, that his hands still trembled. Kit returned to the kitchen, fetched coffee for himself and Avi, placed the fine china cups carefully onto coasters then made himself comfortable on the floor at Avi's feet. Kelly, who had not been inside the house until earlier that morning, looked around admiringly.

"You have a fine collection of antiques, Kester. I would

not have considered that as a side of your character."

Kit laughed but offered no explanation.

"Yeah, there's something I've been meaning to ask you," said Jo. "I thought about it the other day. You've got all this antique stuff in here that you're really fussy about. You know, polish, coasters, the full nine yards. And yet, out in the workshop there's that other table, which is also obviously just as valuable, and you stick those bloody great boots of yours up on it. What gives?"

Kit laughed again.

"You're all wrong. It's not antique, none of it." He paused, thinking. "Well, yeah, I suppose Granddad's stuff is antique by now, I don't know. That table in the workshop's a piece of junk, Jo. It's a practise piece. I made it when I was ten years old. If it falls apart I'll just make another one. It doesn't mean a thing. This stuff, though," he indicated vaguely around the room, "it's different. Most of this was made by Granddad. Oh, I did make that nest of tables and a couple of the chairs there," he pointed to the dining suite. "That was a combined effort."

Jo stared at Kit unbelievingly.

"You made these? All by yourself? You're joking?"

"Nah! I mean... um... no, I'm not joking, yes I made them. Um... well... I made some of them, the things Granddad didn't. Um," Kit floundered. "I'm a cabinet maker. Like... um... I'm qualified. Granddad was a cabinet maker, so when they figured I was too scrambled to stay at school, Granddad took me on as an apprentice." He stopped short, his face flushing red.

"I'm impressed," said Jo. "You never told me that," she levelled at Avi.

"You never asked."

"So, what other hidden talents do you have?" Jo asked Kit.

"None."

"Over there," cut in Avi. "In the cabinet." He directed their attention to a glass-fronted cabinet almost hidden in the front corner of the room. Jo walked over to investigate.

"Wow!" she exclaimed. "Did you make all of these as well?"

"Yeah."

Kelly joined Jo to admire the fine collection of delicately made military models - figures, tanks and armoured cars - which lined the cabinet's shelves.

"See the one in the middle of the third shelf," Avi called over his shoulder. "He won the national competition with that last year."

"I'm impressed," repeated Jo as she and Kelly returned to their chairs. "Kit, you amaze me."

"Well, I'm glad I impress someone," Kit replied. He sighed deeply. "Oh hell! What's going to happen about this bloody tour?"

Mike sipped his coffee.

"Good question."

"I think we grin and bear it," said Kelly. "I don't think we have much of a choice."

"He's got to go." Mike sounded tired but determined.

"Who? Me?" Kit's head shot up.

"No. Danny. I've had enough. There's got to be a way to get rid of him."

"Before the tour?" Jo wasn't impressed.

Mike spread his hands wide in appeal.

"That would be nice, but probably not. Avi, how tight is that contract of his? How can we get out of it?"

"We can't," Avi shook his head. "It's locked up. Watertight. Until after the release of the next single. So we have two choices. We survive the tour as best we can then release that single as fast as is humanly possible, or we pray for an act of divine intervention."

"I'll settle for a lawyer's opinion on his contract," Mike replied.

"I've had one." Avi caught their attention. "Oh yeah," he continued, acknowledging their expressions of surprise, "you lot are way behind. I had a guts full of Danny Gordon months ago. I showed the contract to a colleague of mine who lectures at the university law faculty. I'm sorry, guys, that contract was written up by an expert. We can sack Danny if he's musically incompetent, which he isn't, but we can't sack him just for being an obnoxious prick."

"Damn!" said Mike.

"Get rid of him or I'll kill the bastard."

Kit's statement was delivered very softly but with undeniable finality. He stared up at them from his position on the floor, his blue eyes flashing, his mouth set in a half-smile. Jo noticed his hands were rock steady.

CHAPTER EIGHT

"Hey, take it easy, Kit."

Avi slid forwards in his chair and placed his hands reassuringly on Kit's shoulders. Kit turned his face up, meeting Avi's look of concern with a return stare that was wild but somehow disconnected. Avi strengthened his grip on Kit's bony frame and gradually the wildness retreated, to be replaced again by distressed shaking.

"You didn't mean that, did you?" Avi asked softly.

Kit shook his head.

"I don't know. I think Dr Phillips is right. I won't make the tour. I'm sorry. I can't cope with this any more."

He subsided to rest his head on Avi's knee. Avi stroked Kit's hair to calm him, his eyes beseeching support from the others who remained still, not knowing the right moves and not wishing to make the wrong ones. Avi gently extricated himself from under Kit's head, which slumped even lower to rest on the seat of the chair, and stood up.

"Hang in there a minute," he reassured Kit before striding to the kitchen where he pulled open a cupboard door and snatched up a pill bottle.

Avi muttered an oath when he realised the bottle was empty, then reached for a second, similar bottle. It contained one capsule. Avi muttered another oath, glaring at the bottles as if it was their fault they were empty. He strode back into the lounge, held the offending bottles aloft and demanded of Kit.

"Is this it, then? Is this all you've got left?"

Kit looked up vaguely.

"Yeah."

"Nothing else?"

"Nah." Kit's head fell back onto the chair.

"Shit!"

Avi marched over to the oak sideboard and snatched up the telephone. He skimmed quickly through the personalised numbers in the phone's memory and hit the dial button.

"Gabriel Simmons, please," he snapped crisply to the receptionist who answered.

"I'm sorry," the female voice replied. "Dr Simmons is not on duty at the moment. Can anyone else help?"

Avi didn't bother to answer, merely slammed down the phone and repeated the procedure with a different number. This time a male voice answered.

"Gabriel?" Avi demanded.

"Yes. Who is this?" The voice at the other end was brisk and businesslike.

"Avi Livingstone," Avi supplied.

"Oh." The reply denoted recognition, if not approval.

"It's about Kit's drugs," Avi explained.

"What about them?"

"How come he hasn't got any? Look, Kit's having a really bad time. He's stressed out about as far as he can go and now I find he's got one scungy lithium tablet left and no emergency sedatives! How come?"

"Calm down, Avi." Gabriel Simmons sounded bored. "You sound as if you need the sedatives more than Kester."

"Don't duck-shove the issue." Avi was angry. "You're his bloody doctor, why hasn't Kit got enough medication?"

Gabriel remained controlled. "I am not prepared to discuss this over the telephone."

"Then are you prepared to phone the chemist with a prescription? You phone it in, I'll pick it up."

"No, I am not prepared to do that at all. I'm sorry, Avi, but there are issues here which you are obviously not aware of, but which, I repeat, I am not prepared to discuss over the phone. However, I will compromise. I will be heading into work shortly. I was aware that Kester would be out of lithium tablets by tomorrow and I had intended bringing him some when I come off duty tomorrow morning. But, if it is bothering you that much, I will stop off on my way into work. In the meantime, I would suggest you stop being so emotional, Avi. You will not be helping the situation. Goodbye."

Avi slammed the phone down, frustrated. He wandered disconsolately back to his chair, moved Kit so he could sit down, then manhandled Kit into a position where he could massage the drummer's shoulders in the hope that the contact would act as some sort of palliative.

"I hate to make this day any worse," ventured Mike, "but there's still the police. Are we still going to report these funny phone calls?"

"We have to." Avi stole a quick look down at Kit. "Sorry, mate, there isn't really a choice."

"I'll do it," Mike volunteered.

"Thanks."

Mike's venture on the telephone was more successful than Avi's had been. After being passed through several switchboards, he was finally connected to a youthful-sounding constable who was even more helpful when he realised he was dealing with a member of 'Charlotte Jane'. He said his name was Constable Merata, apologised profusely for the police staffing shortages which left him unable to call round, and politely requested Mike and the others to come into the Central Police Station where he would be only too happy to deal with their complaint personally.

"No problem," Mike reported to the others. "We do have to front up to HQ, though," he said in a fake upper class British accent, adding a mock salute for effect. "It appears they are too short-staffed to send any cars out unless we are being robbed and murdered at this precise moment."

Avi could feel Kit tremble at the prospect of entering the police station. He sought to delay the inevitable, at least until he could get Kit into a more stable frame of mind.

"We can't go until Gabriel's been," he said quickly.

Kit looked up questioningly.

"Gabriel's coming?"

"Yeah. He's bringing some more of your lithium tablets," Avi explained. "And a sedative," he added quietly to himself.

"When?" Mike inquired.

"Um... I don't know exactly," Avi admitted. "On his way to work. What time does he go to work, Kit?"

"I don't know."

"Ring him back and ask him," Jo suggested logically.

Avi hesitated, thinking of Gabriel's unhelpful tone.

"I don't think he'd appreciate that," he said. "Hang on though. Excuse me again, Kit." Avi moved to the phone and dialled swiftly. "Hi," he said to the receptionist who answered, "can you tell me when Dr Simmons is expected in, please?"

"Dr Simmons will be in at four," the female voice replied.

"Thank you," Avi replied politely this time and hung up.

"Four," he relayed back to the others. "He's due there at four so I guess he should be here about half past three."

Mike checked his watch.

"That's an hour away. I could suggest we go do this thing with the police now but, knowing how these things usually go, we'd get horribly held up and miss Gabriel, which is obviously not a good idea." He looked from Avi to Kit who was patently barely aware of his surroundings. "So, how do we fill in an hour?"

"Photos," suggested Jo brightly. She shrugged. "Well, it might cheer Kit up, if nothing else."

"Yeah," agreed Mike, "Why not?"

At Jo's urging the pile of photographs was shifted from the small bedroom to the middle of the lounge floor, the musicians seated around it like excited boy scouts around a camp fire. For the next hour the atmosphere became increasingly lighter as old photographs were passed from hand to hand and ribald comments passed on the looks, fashions and attitudes captured on the celluloid. Even Kit was cajoled into taking an interest although pictures of himself caused him obvious embarrassment. At one stage Jo passed a picture to Mike.

"If that's an example of your taste in clothes, I'm glad you don't dress yourself any more," she teased.

Mike looked at the image and grinned.

"Don't remind me! I was extremely poor in those days. I wore whatever was on special at the op-shop. But, yes, Sarah does have more of a flare for fashion than I do."

"Hey! Wow!" she said later. "This deserves to be put out on permanent display."

"What have you found now?" Avi queried carefully,

unsure if he really wanted to hear the answer.

"Kit," she said lightly. "In a coloured t-shirt, no less."

Kit looked quizzical.

"Well, come on," she goaded. "Find me one other photo in here, or name me one occasion, when you've seen Kit in anything that wasn't black."

The others thought about it then nodded ruefully. Mike looked at the photo.

"I will concede Jo a point, but only just," he said. "It's white with black stripes. Normally I would say that hardly qualifies as coloured, but on Kit I must admit it is fairly riotous."

"Don't you like colour, Kit?" Jo asked.

Kit shrugged.

"Um... I just don't like shopping. Too many decisions. It's not that important." He tailed off into silence, unable to adequately express the mental terrors that accompanied tasks that were a simple pleasure for most people. Jo wouldn't understand.

Jo understood more than Kit realised. She didn't press the issue but, out of a sense of mischief, she stood up and placed the photo in the centre of the mantelpiece.

"There," she said proudly. "Like I said, pride of place."

Just after three thirty there was a sharp rap on the front door. Jo opened it to reveal a stocky, sandy-haired man in his early thirties, not much taller than herself. He was dressed in a well-cut grey double-breasted suit and carried a traditional leather doctor's bag.

"If you're Gabriel, you're expected," she smiled.

"Doctor Gabriel Simmons," he explained, proffering a hand. "And you?"

"Jo Greenwood." His grip was firm, businesslike. "Come in."

Gabriel swept into the room, shaking hands all round and introducing himself to Kelly. Jo thought he reminded her of a politician, or a religious crusader. She also noticed that he ignored Kit. When the pleasantries were concluded, Gabriel placed his bag on the dining table, opened it and pulled out a small phial which he handed to Avi.

"Before you say anything," he said quickly, forestalling Avi's protest as he looked into the phial, "there are only enough pills in there for three days. This is what I want to make quite clear. My brother's condition is deteriorating." He spoke about Kit as if he were not present. "Because of the combination of factors which make up his condition, I consider it would be unwise for him to have access to any larger quantity of drugs at any one time."

"Why?" Jo cut in.

Gabriel eyed her with disdain.

"I am a doctor," he said patiently. "If you were in my position and had a patient who was a drug addict and a depressive with a history of suicide attempts, would you allow that person access to drugs in any great quantity?"

"No, I guess not." Jo couldn't disagree.

"Exactly! When Kester has had access to large supplies of his drugs he has done one of two things. Either he has tried to take them all at once, or he has sold them on the streets to obtain heroin or homebake. Either way he becomes a liability and a damned nuisance, and causes problems for our mother. Plus," Gabriel looked steadily at Avi, "this system allows me to keep a regular check on Kester's condition. There are enough drugs there to last until Monday morning.

I'll call back then." He began to repack his bag, preparatory to leaving.

"Sedatives," Avi demanded. "Take a look at him, Gabriel. Kit is freaking out. He needs a sedative. He is supposed to have a supply of them for emergencies, you know that."

Gabriel glanced at Kit who hadn't left his position on the floor.

"He doesn't look any worse than usual and I am in a hurry."

Avi grabbed Gabriel's arm and swung the young doctor around to face him.

"Then look closer, doctor," he spat. "And listen up. Kit has got some idiot phone caller - probably a fan - calling him at all hours of the night. It's serious, serious enough for us to be talking to the police about it. And on top of that, we've got Danny Gordon throwing hissy fits all over the place and a tour hitting the road in ten, nine now almost, days. For God's sake, Gabriel, Kit needs help!"

"A crank caller? Avi, a word...," he drew Avi after him as he walked towards the front door. Out on the porch he stopped. "Avi, between you and me, I wouldn't put a lot of faith in anything my brother says."

"Are you trying to say he's lying?"

"No. I'm trying to say, in layman's terms and sparing all the text book jargon, he's nuts. Come on, surely you can see it? I'm sorry, I know you two have known each other a long time, but I think you'd better face the facts. My brother is a lost cause. I'll keep him out of hospital as long as I can, mainly for Mum's sake, but ... well... the time is rapidly approaching. Bye."

He was gone before Avi could tell him that he, too, had

heard the phone calls. Avi re-entered the cottage, fuming silently. Kit was still in need of a sedative. Avi picked up the telephone.

"Dr Phillips, please," he asked.

"I'm sorry, Dr Phillips is in a meeting. She won't be available until five o'clock."

Avi put down the phone. "Damn!" He drummed his fingers on the sideboard, thinking, then hurried out to his car and rummaged through the glove box until he found a small brown bottle which he placed in his pocket before returning to the house. There he extracted a tablet which he gave, with a glass of water, to Kit who took it without question.

"It might make you a bit sleepy," Avi explained gently. "But it should make you feel a bit better. Okay?"

"Okay." Kit was trusting. "I didn't think there were any left."

"There weren't," Avi owned up. "I had a secret supply." He took the bottle from his pocket. "Chlorpromazine. Dr Phillips gave me these to carry when we toured, just in case. They were in my car."

"Is that what I had last night?"

"Yeah."

"Good stuff." Kit's speech was already starting to slur. Mike noticed.

"I suggest that we get down to the cop shop and get these statements done before Kit collapses," he suggested.

"You okay?" Avi asked Kit.

"Yeah."

Kit's assertion of control was belied by his staggering gait as he stood up then swayed unsteadily as Avi obligingly leant him a shoulder for support.

By the time the group stood face to face with Constable Rikki Merata Kit was obviously suffering under the influence of the sedative. Unable to stand unaided, he was leaning heavily on Avi, breathing raggedly and blinking glazed and unfocussed eyes. Mike dragged forwards the small office's one spare chair and Avi dumped Kit into it.

"Is he okay?" the constable asked.

"Sedated," Avi explained. "I know it's going to make getting a statement difficult, but he was in such a mess. His brother's a doctor, he came around just before we came down here." Well, it wasn't exactly a lie, just an economical use of the truth.

"So," Constable Merata took up his pen and a position of authority. "What exactly is the problem?"

Technically, it was Kit who should have explained as he was the official complainant, but Avi took over the role, relating the story in much the same way as he had relayed it to the band earlier that day. Rikki Merata took notes. When Avi had finished Merata then asked him to repeat it all over again, but this time into a microphone to record it officially as a statement. Avi sighed heavily but obliged. The band was offered coffee while they waited for the recorded statement to be typed out. Avi and Jo accepted the offer, Mike and Kelly refused and Kit remained unaware that any such offer had been made. Avi and Jo left the others in the small office and followed the constable to the coffee vending machine in the hall. Jo made two coffees while Avi started to light himself a cigarette then stopped as Jo pointed out the no-smoking sign.

"Avi," she said as she handed him his coffee, "can I ask a personal question about Kit?"

Avi shrugged his assent. She could ask, he didn't necessarily have to answer.

"Back at the house, when I was teasing him about wearing black, he was... ah... is he agoraphobic or something?"

"Sort of." Avi drew hard on his cigarette. "Kit has a mental illness, Jo. He's a depressive. He's been sick since he was a kid."

"You're kidding? I didn't think kids could get depression."

"Oh yeah. They can and they do. Personally, I just don't think a lot of them are diagnosed very early. Ask Sarah about it, she specialises in kids."

"Obviously. How many have they got?"

Avi laughed at Jo's blatant attempt to cheer him up.

"Anyway," he continued. "Kit was diagnosed early. Real early. He had his first nervous breakdown at primary school. I can still remember it. The teacher had made us play rugby. Kit and I both hated rugby, neither of us were ever any good at sport. Kit got tackled really hard and after that he wouldn't go near the ball. That just got him into more trouble both with the teacher, who was yelling at him, and the other boys who kept calling him names and pushing him around. After the game he didn't say another word, just sat at his desk and rocked. It wasn't until the bell rang and he still didn't move that they realised something was wrong. He was in hospital for ages." Avi shook his head sadly. "Something disappeared from Kit that day. Some spark of life. It never came back. Sometimes, sometimes when he's behind his drums, you can see it but most of the time... Panic attacks." He broke into his own reverie. "Not agoraphobia really, panic attacks. He can't handle crowds, or decisions. Shopping involves both."

"What about his parents?"

"Huh!" Avi snorted derisively. "Kit's father walked out just after Kit was born. Kit's mother can't stand the sight of him, because he looks like his father and because she may have to explain his illness to her yuppie friends and that would be socially embarrassing. Brother Gabriel, who you met before, looks like Mummy and he's successful, so he's okay. His grandparents were good to him but they're both dead now, so he's pretty much on his own."

"How does he survive? I mean, properties in the Avon Loop cost a fortune, he's got a better car than you've got and, let's face it, 'Charlotte Jane' might have lots of kudos attached but it doesn't pay heaps."

"He inherited the house from his grandparents, likewise the van. Well, his grandfather bought him the van, and he lives on next to nothing. He earns a bit from repairing furniture and he sells a few of the plants and vegetables he grows to the health food shop where Kelly buys his lunch. Damn it! I knew there was something else I wanted to speak to Gabriel about. Kit's money. Apparently Gabriel's handling it at the moment and he seems to be awfully tight-fisted with it. Say, we'd better be getting back."

Avi drained his cup and dropped the rubbish into a convenient receptacle before leading the way back down the corridor to the small office. After what seemed an eternity, the statement was brought in for Avi's signature, along with a second document confirming that the complainant was really one Kester Joseph Simmons, musician, but that, due to the ill-health of said Kester Joseph Simmons, musician, the complaint was being signed in his stead by Avrahim

Jacob Livingstone, musician. Avi signed that as well, after double checking the spelling of his name on both documents.

Mike's watch registered twelve minutes past six when the group piled out of Mike's car and into Kit's house. Kelly offered to tidy up the heap of photographs while Avi helped Kit to bed, but before Avi had reached the bedroom door, Jo gave a startled cry. She was standing, hand outstretched, pointing to the picture of Kit which she had jokingly placed on the mantelpiece only a few hours before.

"Oh my God!"

The picture stood as it had been left, the early band line-up hanging off a large bronze statue of Peter Pan and Wendy, grinning inanely, except Kit's face which had been delicately cut from the photo and now lay on the mantelpiece, pinned in place by one of Kit's sharp scalpel-bladed modelling knives. Kit broke free from Avi, staggered to the fireplace to stare at the bizarre spectacle, swayed drunkenly then fainted.

Over the road, from her vantage point in the Barbadoes Street cemetery, Cassandra Oakleigh watched the proceedings with interest. It had been an amazing day. Things were obviously hotting up for the tour. Danny Gordon had come and gone and come and gone, the woman with the baby, who had to be the wife and child of the only married band member, had come and gone, the dude in the suit had come and gone then the whole band had gone then come.

That had worried her. She could see the keyboard player, the one who had spoken to her at the shop, half carrying her Kester who looked sick. Something wasn't right. He hadn't looked sick when she had touched him at the shop. Sure, he hadn't exactly looked well, either, but he hadn't looked any paler than the Goths who shared her cemetery hang-out.

She thought again of her meeting with Kester Simmons in the hot bread shop. She had touched him. He had touched her. First! Mentally she ran her eyes over him, slowly, piece by piece, instilling forever on her memory his height, his slim frame, his hair, so jet black it was almost blue, and his eyes, so blue they were ... unreal. And now he was sick. Something was wrong. Perhaps she should make sure he was all right. She could go to the door and ask. After all, she could ask, he knew her. She had told him her name. Cassandra made a decision. She left her position in the cemetery and began the meandering walk around the river. When she finally reached the door she was met by a polite but firm Kelly Reynolds.

"Ah!" He said in recognition. "The girl from the shop. No, I'm sorry, you can't speak to Kester. He is unwell and cannot be disturbed."

"What's wrong?"

"Nothing serious," Kelly lied. "He is over-tired and has reacted rather strongly to his medication. It is nothing to be concerned about and it is under control. He is sleeping. However, I shall relay your concern, and good wishes, when he wakes."

Cassandra could see she stood no chance of getting past the bass player, so she trounced off, muttering "stuck-up yuppie" under her breath as she left.

Kelly, who heard, sniggered to himself as he shut the door. He paused as a fleeting thought dashed across his brain but failed to materialise. He tried to recall it, failed, shrugged and passed it off as meaningless, returning to Avi,

Mike and Jo who sat quietly in the lounge.

"That was the young lady from the bread shop, the one with the fancy for Kester. I told her Kester was ill but it was nothing serious."

"We heard," said Jo.

"What do we do now?"

"What else can we do?" Mike asked. "I mean, we've rung Constable Merata and reported the photo. We can't drag Kit back to the police station, he's done in."

"Or spaced out," Jo corrected.

"That, too," Mike agreed. "Still, he's out for the count. Look, Avi, it's up to you. I'm going to have to go home at some stage. Will you stay with Kit?"

"Yeah. I'll be in deep trouble with my parents but I guess it can't be helped. They can like it or lump it. Yeah, you guys go home. Get some sleep. I'll stay with Kit and we'll sort it out in the morning."

"Will you be all right here?"

"Yeah. I'll lock up real tight and I'll rip the phone out. I'm not taking any of those damned crank calls. Go on, get out of here. I'll see you tomorrow."

After playing with his daughters and tucking them into bed, Mike made an apology to his wife and headed into the privacy of the office he had set up in the front room of his house. He unlocked the filing cabinet, pulled out a file and picked up the phone. It was a private line running only to the office so he knew he would not be overheard when he made his call.

"It's Mike," he said as the call was answered. "It's time. It has to be now. After the tour is too late, we have to act right now. You got the contract I sent you? Great. It's over to you now. Just do it quickly."

Danny Gordon was angry. He had been pumping iron for two hours. He could have done another hour before the gym closed but that other young prick who thought he was better than Danny had started an argument and they had both been told to leave. So he was sitting in the local pub, drinking beer and planning revenge.

Down the road, only a few blocks from Cassandra Oakleigh's flat, Danny's competition opened the door to his garage, flicked on the lights to reveal an impressive array of weight-lifting equipment and stepped forwards to his favourite machine. He placed his hands firmly on the bar of the weight, pushed it into the air, grunted at the effort and, as he exercised, planned his revenge.

Kit's sleep was plagued with strange and surreal images. Somewhere, away in the distance, but close by, there was Avi. There were swirling colours and large, hairy insects with bright red hair. There were feet, an army of feet, huge black hairy insect feet, marching up and down the gravel driveway outside his window. There was Danny Gordon, shouting and Avi, shouting back, then a spider, still with red hair, in a denim jacket, crawling up his arm. He thrashed around, wildly, trying to get rid of the spider but it wouldn't let him go. It hung on to his arm, stroking at his hair with its horrid hairy feet and talking to him in Avi's voice, telling him not to worry. Then it started to eat his face. Kit woke, screaming.

Avi comforted him, holding him tight until he slept again,

peacefully this time. The next time he woke daylight was streaming in through the window and Avi was sitting on the edge of the bed, smiling encouragement and offering him breakfast.

"I have to go home for a bit," he said gently. "Will you be okay?"

"Why?"

"I have to placate the parents. It's Friday so the Sabbath starts tonight and I was supposed to help Dad cut some firewood before then. Plus I have to tell Mum that Danny expects us to rehearse tomorrow so I won't be at Chapel or the Sabbath meal. They are not going to like that."

"So tell them by phone."

"No. I have to go home. Just for an hour. It's quarter to nine now. Rehearsal starts at ten. By the time you've eaten breakfast and had a shower the others'll be arriving. I'll be back before you notice. Anyway, I need some clean clothes. These are starting to walk by themselves. Okay?"

"Okay."

"One thing before I go. Money, Kit. We were going to talk about it last night, remember? But we didn't get around to it."

Kit nodded his head, there was a vague memory of it somewhere in his head, just not right at the front.

"We still have to talk about it," Avi pressed. "I don't want to hassle you, so if you can just tell me how much allowance you're getting from Gabriel, I'll do some quick budget calculations and we'll go over them together later."

"Fifty," said Kit.

"Fifty?" Avi repeated incredulously. "Fifty dollars! Are you telling me Gabriel expects you to live on only fifty dollars a week?"

"Yeah, but he pays the power, the phone and the rates first."

"Oh, big deal! Kit, you're being ripped off. You're expected to buy food, clothes, run your van, everything, on fifty dollars? That's ridiculous. Where's the rest of the money going?"

"There isn't any."

"Oh rubbish! Look, I know you don't earn heaps, but even with power, phone and rates taken off, there's still got to be more than fifty dollars left."

Kit's bony shoulders lifted in a resigned shrug.

"Gabriel says that's all there is."

"What about the band money? The royalties and the gig payments?"

Kit shrugged again.

"I don't know. Ask Gabriel."

Avi gave up but resolved to call on Doctor Gabriel Simmons later that day and have a very long talk.

"Okay," he said more cheerfully than he felt. "I've got to go. I'll be back soon, I promise."

Avi revved life into his aged Toyota and eased it out of the driveway. As he swung into Oxford Terrace he noticed Danny's vivid green Charger parked by the river.

"Damn," he thought. "I forgot to tell Kit Danny was here late last night. Back early this morning, and quietly, I didn't hear him come in."

He drove away remembering Daniel's arrival at about ten o'clock the previous night. Avi had heard the noise and crept out, thinking it was their phantom caller, only to run into a drunk and belligerent Danny who had pushed Avi roughly out of the way, telling him to mind his own business and go back to his boyfriend. Avi knew Danny had intended to fix Mike's damaged amplifier. As the car was back early this morning, Avi could only assume that Danny had been too drunk to complete the repairs and had sneaked back this morning to finish the job before anyone, notably Avi himself, could pass any comments.

CHAPTER NINE

The early morning traffic was heavy as Avi coaxed his reluctant vehicle from the central city towards Beckenham in the south. The elderly car didn't take kindly to sitting ungaraged and undriven for two nights and was refusing to fire on all cylinders. The trip down the one-way system was fraught with problems as the car stalled at each intersection then had to be cajoled back into life amid tooting, taunting and abuse from other road users. Avi, in increasing frustration, fuelled by exhaustion and an honest knowledge of his own mechanical ineptitude, resorted to tactics he normally considered far below his dignity - he swore back, raising his fingers in an obscene gesture of rebuke.

The car coughed and wheezed its way slowly over the Waltham overbridge, under which the remains of the city's once-proud railway network still thrust rusting tentacles, going nowhere. The downhill side of the bridge gave the Toyota an extra burst of energy which carried it relatively trouble-free down Waltham Road, past the outdoor swimming pool where he and Kit spent many hours as children, and around the banks of the Heathcote River, to swing finally into the driveway of his parents' 1930's styled weatherboard bungalow.

Avi pulled the car to a stop on the neat double strips of concrete, aware that his car would probably drop oil on the identically spaced row of tiny pansies which his mother had carefully planted in the plot of dirt that lay between the strips. He wondered why she bothered. As the car's brakes ended their distinctive squeal, Avi sat back, suddenly aware of the tension with which he had been gripping the steering wheel, egging the car home by sheer will power. He forced his fingers to release their determined grip, flexed them several times to restore mobility, then ran his hands through the matted rat-tails that were forming in his long, unbrushed hair. Dreading the outcome, he forced himself to study his image in the rear view mirror. As expected, the sight revolted him. In spite of his penchant for old, tatty - comfortable, lived-in, he called them - jeans, Avi's usual style did not include sweat-stained clothes that had been slept in, twice, a now three-day growth of beard and hair that would soon qualify him to play reggae.

Avi climbed out of his car and approached the house from the back. He was sincerely hoping to avoid his mother, at least until after he had cleaned himself up. He walked around the side of the house and entered through the back door into the laundry area. The automatic washing machine chugged mechanically in one corner and a pile of neatly folded towels warned Avi that his mother was already well into her Sabbath preparations. This was confirmed by the rich smell of baking that wafted to meet him as he opened the door into the kitchen. He paused for a moment, preparing his story in advance - he was bound to meet his mother on his way through to his room. Avi took a deep breath, steeled himself and stepped into the kitchen. His father's fist struck him full in the face.

He reeled back, blood gushing as his nose splintered under the hammer force of the blow. He staggered backwards into the laundry, followed by his father, striking blows with the precision of a prize fighter. Jacob Livingstone was a big man, an inch shorter than Avi's five feet eleven inches, but he carried at least thirty kilograms more weight than his son and he had the advantage of surprise. He struck again. As Avi collapsed against the washing machine, he had the ludicrous realisation that he was bleeding all over his mother's clean towels. He sank to the floor, an arm raised across his face in futile protection against the savage rain of blows. In the background he could hear his mother's voice, screaming.

"No, Jacob! No!"

Jacob Livingstone thrust aside Avi's outstretched arm, hauled his son to his feet by the lapels of his faded plaid shirt and half dragged him into the kitchen, slamming him up against the hard edge of the clinically clean stainless steel bench. He slapped Avi's face again, for good measure, then stood back, panting with the effort. Avi braced himself against the bench, eyes welling with tears of pain and humiliation, lungs gasping as he choked on the blood that ran thickly from his broken nose. Hazily, through the fading sight of an already swelling black eye, he could see his mother, cowering in the opposite corner, hugging her apron protectively to her bosom. He raised his arm, using his sleeve to wipe away some of the blood from his face, and choked back a wave of nausea. Jacob stepped forwards again, rocking Avi's face with another savage open-handed slap.

"You filthy little pervert!" the older man screamed. "How dare you call yourself a son of mine!"

"Jacob! Please!" Elizabeth Livingstone begged for her son.

Jacob swung round to glare at his wife, who cowered back further into the far corner. His father's movement gave Avi just enough room to inch away slightly and regain his balance. By the time Jacob swung back, Avi was breathing raggedly, but poised to strike back.

"You were with him, weren't you?" Jacob ranted. "You disgust me! You're an abomination! How dare you come back here! How dare you soil your mother's house!"

"You're sick!" Avi spat back. "I don't know what you're talking about."

He pushed away from his father and took refuge behind the small table that stood in the centre of the kitchen. Jacob squared off against him from the other side of the table.

"Yes you do," he snarled. "You know exactly what I mean. You and that... that thing! You spent the last two nights at his house. Don't think we don't know. I saw your car in his driveway. I saw it with my own eyes."

"You don't understand."

"I understand only too well." Jacob approached Avi menacingly. "I warned you what I would do if I ever caught you with him."

Avi backed off, keeping the table firmly between himself and his father. His mind was racing now with genuine fear. His memories raced back ten years to a similar scene. A thirteen year old Avi, even more terrified than the adult one now was, his mother, just as hysterical with fear and torn loyalties, and his father, shouting and berating, quoting from the Bible and waving Avi's diary, the incriminating evidence of two young boys' experiments verified in black and white, in Avi's own youthful writing.

"I can see you remember." Jacob's tone was cold. "Let's see how well you play your precious piano now, boy!"

"No!"

Avi made a break for the door but got no further than the end of the table. Jacob moved fast, catching his son in the side of the head with another roundhouse blow. Avi's knees buckled under him and he sank to the floor. Jacob hauled Avi's unconscious form onto a kitchen chair, allowing Avi's head to hit the table with heavy thud. He glared defiantly at his wife, daring her to intervene but fear held her in her corner, sobbing and clutching her apron to her own badly bruised face. Avi came to. He lifted his head slowly, trying desperately to register through the thick pea soup that was his brain. An attempt to move brought his father's huge hands down on his shoulders, forcing him back into the chair.

"Don't try it," Jacob growled.

"Do as he says," Elizabeth begged.

"It's not what you think," Avi pleaded. "Please listen."

"I've done with listening." Jacob began to pace the floor. "I've listened to you two for years, your pathetic stories about how that boy was really a nice kid," he spat out the words with venom. "Nice kid, be damned! He's just like his father, another filthy pervert. Listen! I've listened for too long. I should have taken action, not listened to your wishy-washy rubbish and your poncey, intellectual friends."

"Dad, please!"

"Don't speak to me! You've disgraced me, you've disgraced your mother. Don't make matters worse by lying. We know you've spent the last two nights at his house. In his bed!"

"No, Dad, honestly! It wasn't like that, Kit was sick."

A vicious slap knocked Avi sideways.

"Don't mention that name in my house!" Jacob's voice dropped to an ominous hush, "We made a bargain, you and I, when you were thirteen, didn't we?"

Dread spread ice-cold through Avi's veins, racking him with shivers of panic. He didn't answer.

"I, at least, keep my promises," his father continued.

He reached out suddenly and grabbed Avi's right hand. Avi struggled to free himself but his father was much stronger. Tears now flowed freely down Avi's face, mixing with the blood that stained his shirt front and splashed on the table. Avi knew his father's intentions and begged for mercy.

"Please, please. Not my hands, not my hands."

Elizabeth started to move forwards to help her son but fell back under the wrathful gaze of her husband. Jacob held his son's long-fingered delicate hand for close scrutiny.

"Look at you," he said scornfully. "You look like a girl with your long hair and your pretty hands. Like you pretty, does he? Well it wasn't a girl baby we christened twenty three years ago. It was a son! I'm glad the Preacher isn't here to see you now, he would be so ashamed. It's all her fault," he threw his wife a scornful glare, "All that rubbish about sending you to public schools to make sure you fitted in, how difficult it would be for you if you were singled out as being different. I had a son once, a son I hoped would grow into a man I could be proud of, a man doing a man's job, not wasting his time playing music like some feckless schoolgirl."

Avi was too afraid to speak. Jacob's voice dropped even lower.

"There'll be no more music!"

With one strong hand Jacob Livingstone pinned his son's right hand to the kitchen table. Avi saw his father's other hand rise, his mother's steak tenderising mallet held aloft. He screamed as the mallet crashed down and the bones in his hand shattered.

Jacob dragged his son's limp body from the kitchen out into the laundry. To the right of the entrance was an old-fashioned wooden door, painted the same subdued apricot as the laundry walls. Jacob opened the door and threw Avi through it into a tiny, windowless, wardrobe-sized space that had once served as a receptacle for coal. He slammed the door shut and clicked into place a huge brass padlock. From a hook on the wall he took the padlock keys which he waved purposefully in front of his wife.

"Just so you don't get any ideas," he sneered as he dropped the keys into his pocket.

"You can't leave him in there," Elizabeth sobbed. "Please. Jacob, don't do this!"

"It's done," her husband declared. "He can stay there a while. It'll give him time to think."

"But his hand! Please, he needs a doctor."

"I don't care. He should have thought of that before. He stays where he is. There'll be plenty of time for doctors later, when he's learned some manners."

Jacob Livingstone pushed his wife back into the kitchen where he waved a hand airily at the blood that lay in pools on the bench and the table and ran in smeared streaks down the white-painted cupboards under the bench and across the apricot vinyl floor tiles.

"Clean this mess up!" he ordered. "Then make me a cup of tea. I'm going to read the newspaper."

Fully confident he would be obeyed, Jacob Livingstone marched through to the front of the house and settled himself comfortably in his favourite chair. Things were now as he wished them to be. His wife would run a tidy house which would be admired by his friends when they visited and his son would now get a respectable job and take his proper place in society. After a nice, refreshing cup of tea he would phone his work to explain his absence that day due to a family problem, then he would phone his old friend, Adam Hennessy. Adam had recently scored a large building contract, and he owed Jacob a favour. There would be a proper job there for Avrahim.

In the kitchen Elizabeth Livingstone cried silent tears into the bucket as she cleaned away the blood.

Jo jumped as the car tooted behind her then relaxed as she recognised Mike's grinning face behind the wheel.

"Get in!" he shouted as the white car pulled into the kerb.

"I'm not that lazy," Jo expostulated, but she got in nevertheless. "It's only one block!"

"So what?" Mike eased the car back into the Madras Street traffic, indicating for a right turn into the two-way stretch of Kilmore Street that led into the Avon Loop.

"Don't you live at Riccarton?" Jo asked as she buckled her seatbelt.

"Yeah."

"Then aren't you going the wrong direction?"

"I'm going to Kit's, I thought that was the right direction."

"Oh, you know what I mean. Aren't you coming from the wrong direction? I thought you came into the Loop from Barbadoes Street."

"Guilty," Mike grinned conspiratorially. "Shhh, don't tell."

Jo shook her head in mock despair.

"I know," she said. "Shut up, Jo, mind your own business."

Mike laughed and pulled the car to a halt beside Danny's Charger.

"Oh oh!" he grimaced. "He got here before us. And here was I thinking I'd be bright and early and earn some Brownie points."

"You too?"

"Must be a common complaint." Mike pointed up the road to where Kelly's mountain bike was just coming into view around the winding Loop.

Jo had joined Kelly across the road by the time Mike had hauled his guitar case from the back seat and locked his car. Kelly chained his bike to the fence and the three musicians made their way up the driveway to the back of the house.

"I thought Avi was staying here last night," said Jo.

"He was," Mike agreed.

"His car's not here."

Mike shrugged. "He's probably gone out for cigarettes."

"Probably," Jo agreed. "It's awfully quiet. House or workshop?"

"House," Mike voted. "If Avi isn't here and Danny is, I suggest we find Kit and stand between them."

"I gather you are also predicting another stormy day, Michael," Kelly drawled.

"Anyone who doesn't wins the 'Optimist-of-the-week' award." Mike opened the back door to let them in. "You're right, Jo, it is awfully quiet."

The house appeared to be empty. Dirty dishes in the sink suggested there had been some life, but any other traces of it were absent. Mike and Kelly placed their guitars carefully on the floor and looked around. Mike put his head around the door of the spare bedroom then backed out, shrugging a negative reply to Jo's unspoken question. He moved to the main bedroom, peeked around the door then beckoned to the others. Kit was asleep, limbs and hair sprawled in all directions, his breakfast cold and uneaten, abandoned on the dresser. Mike leant against the door post, arms folded, head cocked to one side.

"Idyllic, isn't it?"

"If I had something on my bed that was all legs and hair like that, I'd spray it with fly killer," Jo laughed. "Come on, Kit," she shook him none-too-gently. "Wakey, wakey!"

Kit stirred and murmured but didn't wake.

"Kit!" Jo shook him harder. "Come on, man! Wake up! Danny is out in the workshop. If he finds you still asleep he'll have your guts for a guitar string!"

Kit struggled to open his eyes. With difficulty he hauled himself up onto his elbow and blinked with a distinct lack of comprehension. Mike recognised the symptoms.

"Oh hell!" he muttered. "He's still stoned. Great!"

"What?" Jo sounded incredulous. "From last night? Surely not?"

"Yeah." Mike stooped to look hard into Kit's eyes. "Yeah, trust me. He's still out of it."

"No, no," Kit protested feebly. "I'm okay. I'll be fine, honest. Just give me some time."

"Coffee?" suggested Jo.

"Oh, yes, please." Kit's gratitude was unfeigned. He looked around, focussing more clearly. "Where's Avi?"

"We figured you'd tell us," said Mike. "His car isn't here."

"Oh." Kit's vague answer indicating that he hadn't really grasped Mike's statement.

"Hell and damnation!" Mike swore in frustration. "Kelly,

you can forget that optimist award, it just went right out the window. If we even make it to lunch time we'll be doing damn well! Kit!" He shook the drummer vigorously enough to elicit a whimper of protest. "Come on, let's get you sorted out. Jo, please, make coffee for all of us. Black, very strong. Kelly, if you can give me a hand here we'll throw Kit under a shower."

The two men grabbed an arm each and hoisted Kit to his feet.

"I'm okay, really," he protested but he still leant heavily on their shoulders as they led him through to the bathroom.

It was a more-together Kit who appeared from the bathroom ten minutes later, wrapped decorously in a white towel. He grinned sheepishly at Jo and blushed.

"You look better clean-shaven," Jo reached over and tweaked the edge of the towel. "The colour suits you."

"Yeah, sure." Kit didn't sound as bright as he looked.

"Hey," she called after his retreating back, "Kit! Let me guess, the underwear's black too, huh?"

Kit spun round, clutching his towel deliberately in place.

"You want to come and find out?"

"Is that a threat or a promise?"

"Um," Kit laughed nervously. "A pretty scary thought, actually."

"Get some clothes on then, or I might lose control."

"Yeah, sure."

Kit ambled into his room, reappearing seconds later in his traditional black and dragging a comb through long hanks of wet hair. Jo thrust a cup of coffee towards him.

"Here! Say, Kit, where is Avi?"

Kit shrugged, spilling hot coffee over his hand as he did

so, swore, put the cup down hurriedly and wiped the hot liquid off onto his jeans.

"I don't know," he answered, checking his hand for damage. "I really don't know."

"Think carefully." Mike tried employing tactics he had watched Sarah use on the children. "He stayed the night, yes?"

"Yeah."

"So he must have gone out this morning."

"Yeah." Kit was concentrating hard.

"He must have made breakfast. There are dirty plates in the sink, obviously his, and yours is still by the bed. Think. Can you remember Avi bringing you breakfast?"

Kit closed his eyes, running scenes through his memory.

"Home," he said at last. "He was going home. And something about money, I can't remember."

"Maybe he was going to the bank?" Jo suggested.

"Maybe."

Mike checked his watch. "Well, he'd better be back soon. It's after ten o'clock. Danny won't appreciate it if we get a late start. You did know he was out there already, Kit?"

"No."

"Well, he did intend to fix the amplifier," Kelly reminded them. "No doubt that is what he is doing."

"Oh well," sighed Jo. "I suppose I could show my loving and forgiving nature and offer the man a cup of coffee, couldn't I?"

"You could, if you had one," agreed Kelly.

Jo treated him to a disdainful glare, pulled another cup from the cupboard and reached for the coffee. Mike put his cup down and pulled two sheets of paper from his pocket.

"Before I forget," he said to Kit. "This arrived on my office fax last night. The cover sheet is addressed to Mike Kiesanowski, spelt with two 'e's and a 'v' instead of a 'w', and says 'please on-pass this to Kester Simmons. Must reach him soonest. Please advise if unable to comply.' Then follows an enigmatic text that reads like a James Bond script. Listen to this." Mike cleared his throat and quoted from the second of the two pages. "Must conclude deal soonest. Flying in Friday. Guarantee cash transaction if merchandise satisfactory. Commission assured. K.B." Mike handed the papers to Kit. "More Secret Squirrel stuff, eh?"

Kit took the papers and read the message again, his face slowly registering a broad smile. He folded the papers and placed them on the breakfast bar with a shake of his head.

"Yeah, thanks for taking the message. I really appreciate it."

Mike looked at him with suspicion but said nothing.

"On guard, boys," said Jo cheerfully. "I'm off to slay the dragon."

The men heard Jo's light-hearted giggle as she sauntered jauntily down the yard to the workshop. Then the laugh quickly choked off into a piercing scream. The three men moved as one, downing coffee cups and racing to the workshop. Kelly reached the scene first. By the time Mike and Kit arrived, Kelly was holding Jo tightly, the two of them standing in a pool of blood. Kit took one look and stumbled weakly back against the door.

"Oh my God," he gasped.

In front of him his precious Tama drum kit was a mess. The snare, still locked on its individual stand, was lying on the floor, its skins slashed and its maple shell split open. The row of toms were still mounted on their metal rack but showed various amounts of damage, from the little eight inch which was dangling, skins slashed and mounting twisted, to the sixteen inch which had suffered a single gash. It was impossible to see the damage to the bass drum as it was partially covered by the slumped body of Danny Gordon.

CHAPTER TEN

Detective Inspector Brian Rossiter added his car to the increasing line-up of traffic parked on the picturesque riverbank. An all-encompassing glance took in the surrounding scene. He smiled with satisfaction. Only half an hour had elapsed since the Christchurch Central Police Station had taken the call and already the two attending 'I' cars had the property sealed off. His mouth twisted into a wry grin as he surveyed the inquisitive neighbours gathering in hushed clumps, speculating on the reason for the hastily erected fence of plastic string that now barred entry to the Simmons property. Rossiter waved away a dishevelled young man in jeans and a tweed sports jacket, his fair head enveloped in the folds of an ancient university scarf, who had rushed forwards from one of the watching groups.

"Not now, Mr Bennett," Rossiter snapped. "I can hardly tell you anything I don't know myself. Bloody press!" he muttered under his breath as he stepped over the cordon. "Watch that one," he said to the constable on duty at the end of the driveway, indicating the fair young man. "That's Bennett from 'The Press'. Don't tell him anything."

"Yes, Sir," the constable acknowledged. "The body's not in the house, Sir. It's in a shed at the back," he added helpfully.

"Thank you, Constable." The Detective Inspector let his breath out slowly in a resigned sigh and turned to the young journalist. "Got all that, Bennett?"

Nick Bennett returned a gracious smile and an obsequious bow. The detective scowled and turned on his heel, muttering under his breath as he walked away. Rossiter continued to the rear of the house where he found a small knot of people accompanied by a policewoman. A girl stood, crying, comforted by the policewoman and by a young man with short, spiky hair. Another young man, long haired this time, sat huddled and rocking against the side of the house, comforted in his turn by the last of the group, a man in his late twenties, long haired and moustached.

"Which one of you found the body?" Rossiter asked.

"I did," the girl replied shakily.

"Where is it?"

"In there, Sir." The policewoman pointed to the workshop.

"Wait here, you lot. Don't touch anything."

Rossiter walked determinedly into the workshop, careful not to disturb the scene by his movements. Detective Senior Sergeant John Matheson, the Officer In Charge (Site), was already there, studiously searching the floor around the smashed drum kit. Rossiter looked at the body which still lay at the front of the bass drum.

"Who was he?" he asked.

"Daniel McKay Gordon." Matheson stood up, brushing dust from his portly frame. "They're a rock band. Apparently he sang and played guitar."

"Any idea how he died?" Rossiter removed an expensive pair of German-framed spectacles from his nose with one hand and with the other extracted from his pocket a huge handkerchief with which he set about furiously polishing the spectacle lenses; an automatic habit when he was thinking.

"Looks like a stabbing. There's a sizeable gash in his chest."

"Weapon?"

"Haven't found one yet."

"Who are those guys out there?" He replaced his glasses.

"The rest of the band. The girl, Joanna Greenwood, found the body when she went to invite him in for a cup of coffee. The bloke in the plaid shirt, Michael Something-or-other-sounded-foreign, reported it. The tall, skinny one in black is Kester Simmons. He owns this place, and the damaged drums."

"Simmons! Of course!" Rossiter struck his head with his hand in a gesture of recognition. "I thought he looked familiar. Okay, you carry on here. I'll get this lot down to the station and get some statements. And don't worry," he called back over his shoulder, "I'll handle Bennett."

Rossiter walked briskly back to the small group still huddled by the back door of the house.

"Right, Constable," he addressed the policewoman. "Let's get these people down to the station."

"What for?" Mike broke in.

"We need your statements, Sir," Rossiter addressed him politely.

"Why can't we do that here? Why do we have to go to the station?"

"The whole place is now a crime scene. We can't risk contaminating it," Rossiter explained. "And it's much easier down at the station. If you would be so kind."

He gently but firmly ushered the group into motion. Mike put out a hand to pull Kit to his feet.

"No!" Kit resisted. "No! I don't want to go!"

Rossiter stepped forwards, knelt down and placed a firm hand on Kit's shoulder.

"Mr Simmons. We need to know what happened. It will

be a lot easier on everyone if you do this voluntarily"

"Come on, Kit," Mike urged. "We're all going. It'll be okay."

"But what about Avi? He'll be back soon. He won't know where we've gone."

"Back" Rossiter's ears pricked up. "You mean there was someone else here?"

"Yeah," Kit replied. "Avi."

"Avi who?" Rossiter asked. "When was he here? Why did he leave?"

"Avi Livingstone," Mike took over the explanation. "Kit hasn't been well. Avi stayed here with him last night but he wasn't here when we arrived. I gather he's gone to his own home and is coming back shortly. We were supposed to be rehearsing so he won't be long."

"Rehearsing. So he's part of the band then?"

"Yeah, sorry. He plays keyboard. Danny would never admit it but Avi's really the band leader."

Rossiter filed that piece of information away to add to his questions later and smiled reassuringly. "Don't worry, the constable at the gate will tell him where you are. Come on. The sooner we do it, the shorter time it will take."

"But my drums," Kit protested weakly.

"Forget them for now. You can't do anything about them at the moment. Come on!"

Mike hauled Kit to his feet and led him away. Jo and Kelly followed, shepherded by Brian Rossiter in the direction of one of the 'Central I' cars. As the group was driven away, Rossiter was again approached by Dominic Bennett.

"Mr Bennett!" Rossiter forestalled the journalist's question. "At this stage all I can tell you is that a body has been discovered in a shed at the rear of this property. The name of the deceased cannot be revealed until the next of kin have been notified."

"The car that just drove away contained all of 'Charlotte Jane' except for Danny Gordon and Avi Livingstone," Bennett pressed. "Is the body either of them?"

Rossiter shook his head. "No comment!"

He brushed away Bennett's attentions and hurried back to the workshop where he found Matheson again on hands and knees searching carefully among the sound equipment. Matheson started at Rossiter's approach, the involuntary movement eliciting an amused snigger from the senior officer.

"Sorry to startle you, John," he apologised with a smile. "I know I said I was going but I want your opinion before I go."

"Sure!" Matheson got to his feet. "How can I help?"

"Our old friend, Simmons. How did he appear to you?"

"That's the guy who owns this place?" Matheson shrugged. "Pretty upset, actually. Mind you, that's fairly understandable." He paused, thinking. "No, I have to admit, it did strike me that all his panic was about his drums. I don't think he'd even noticed that his mate was dead. You seem to know the guy. Should I?"

"No, probably not. He hasn't been in trouble for a few years now. He'd go back before your time here. He's a regular outpatient at Sunnyside Hospital and a drug addict from way back. We caught him a few times selling his medication to buy heroin. He was let off lightly the first couple of times but the third time the magistrate wasn't so understanding. I gather prison life kicked him where it hurt."

"Had a hard time, did he?"

"So I heard, but it straightened him out a bit. He hasn't gone off the rails since."

"Are you considering him a likely suspect for this little lot, then?"

"It's a strong possibility. It's his house. They're his drums. And he did seem extremely reluctant to go down to the station. Put it this way, I'll be questioning him personally. Any luck on a weapon yet?"

"No. I've got a team coming in to search the grounds."

"You might try the river as well."

"I intend to if the grounds come up blank."

"Okay, carry on. I'll see you later."

Rossiter sauntered back to his car, noticing with relief that Nick Bennett was safely employed questioning the neighbours who were still hovering outside. With movements kept deliberately slow, Rossiter unlocked his car, climbed in then made a show of looking busy while he studied the various bystanders. They seemed a typical cross-section of Avon Loop residents, the elderly who had been in the area all their lives and the greenie-hippy-liberal types who had flocked to the area in recent years. Rossiter sighed. Somehow, based on his past experiences, he didn't expect much useful information to be forthcoming from either group. He expected it would be even more difficult to extract anything voluntarily from any of the third group of watchers, however he took a long look at the group of young Goths who were watching from the safety of the cemetery on the other side of the river and made a mental note to try them anyway. As he drove away he realised that one of the group, a trashy young girl with flaming red hair, was studying him with equal intensity.

Keeping his movements as slow and gentle as possible, Avi dragged himself into a corner of the tiny room. Very carefully he managed to ease his body around until he was leaning against the rough wooden side of the old coal container. By the time he had achieved his goal he felt nauseous and faint. For a few minutes he sat desperately trying to control both his ragged breathing and his mounting panic.

He couldn't see; a combination of the windowless room, a blackened eye now completely swollen and closed and the lack of his glasses, lost with his father's first blow. Avi hated the dark and he hated the coal shed. His father had used this punishment on him many times when he was a child and it had never failed to terrify him. Frankly, being shut anywhere in the dark terrified him and the young Avrahim would do anything to avoid it. However, that had been years ago and Avi Livingstone, BA BMus, had outgrown all those childish fears, hadn't he?. He had spent many, many hours helping Kit conquer his fears and he considered himself something of an expert in stripping them down to the basics and looking at them logically. So why was he scared stiff here in the dark?

He hurt. Every movement brought fresh waves of pain, from the dull, drum-beat throbbing that encircled his head in a vicious band to the sharp, searing knives of agony that tore from his smashed right hand through his arm and into his central nervous system, bringing with them their attendant waves of nausea and fainting.

He wondered what the time was. He had no idea how long he had been there. How long had he been unconscious? Surely the others would miss him soon. Rehearsals must have started by now. He had a watch but it was on his left arm and, in order to see it in the dark, he would have to push the tiny button on the side with his right hand. Moving his right hand was out of the question. A moment's thought then Avi gingerly cradled his right hand with his left, lifting the injured limb onto his lap. The effort was immense and brought him out in another bout of cold sweat. After a few minute's rest, he tried again, moving his left hand to his right and laboriously working the tiny buttons on the watch. The effort paid off and through the gloom he could just make out the little digital message − 11.17. A fresh wave of nausea forced him back to rest against the rough-hewn wood of the coal box. He tried to focus his gaze through the blackness but he could see nothing. A deep gulp swallowed his rising fear.

"Cool it, Avi. Just keep calm."

He knew talking to himself didn't amount to much practical help, but any sort of noise was mentally reassuring. He forced himself to pull back into focus memories that he had spent years trying to erase. To be shut in the coalhouse was the ultimate punishment, his father's favourite method of discipline. His father was a cruel man, stern, old fashioned and unbending. The conservative tunnel vision through which he viewed the world had no room to fit understanding of the dreamy, musical thoughts that drove his wife and only child. Avi was supposed to grow up to fulfil his father's idea of a real man. He conceded his father must have been bitterly disappointed.

"So! What's the solution?"

From his university studies Avi could appreciate that the concept of putting a naughty child into a quiet space to consider their actions had some merit, it was just a pity that his father had inadvertently chosen the one place that would trigger Avi's one and only phobia. Mind you, Avi shuddered as an involuntary movement of his hand caused another searing wave of pain, the theory didn't usually involve half killing them first!

Avi lay back, cradling his injured hand. Yeah, he could see his father's point of view, even if he could not condone, and would never forgive, the vicious attack he had just been through. His parents' world revolved heavily around correct social behaviour. There was a right way to live, which involved keeping both house and person neat, tidy and well-groomed, and he could see how his own scruffy appearance and alternate outlook must have given his father cause for many sleepless nights. However, if he had inherited anything from his father, it was his single-minded determination. It was his life and he'd live it how he chose. He let out a deep sigh.

"Livingstone," he said aloud, "I think it's time to leave home." He pulled himself into a more upright position. "Let's set some priorities here. Number one, how do I get out of here? That should be simple. If I can get it out of my pocket, I'll phone them." With his left hand he reached around to his hip pocket. At first he was puzzled by the lack of the solid outline of the phone through the denim, then with a feeling of utter hopelessness he remembered leaving it in his jacket – back at Kit's. "Oh fuck!" he swore as panic started to take over. "Calm down. Think. Okay, logic says that they will have noticed that I am not at rehearsal and, by now, Danny will be throwing hissy fits in all directions. So surely somebody, even among that lot, will have had the common sense to ring Mum and see where I am. Then she will have to let me out. Anyway, she's bound to let me out at lunch time. Then I suppose they will expect me to apologise. Oh well, it's only words, sort of like singing country and western music - you only have to sing all the right words in the right key, but you don't have to feel the sentiment. As long as I can get to a doctor. Oh hell, Danny's going to kill me."

With another pained sigh, Avi slumped back again. From the house he could hear sounds of movement but they seemed too quiet. On a Friday the house would normally have been filled with joyful sounds. It was a day his mother usually enjoyed, as if preparing for the Sabbath was her own personal celebration. She should have been singing. Avi loved to hear his mother sing. She had a strong, pure voice and an innate sense of feeling and Avi had always believed it was from her that he had inherited his musical abilities. Certainly it was his mother who had fostered them. But today there was no singing, just the muffled sounds of shuffling feet and tentative household duties.

"Oh, please, Mum, let me out!"

"Air New Zealand announces the departure of flight NZ279 to Invercargill. Passengers please board at Gate Nine."

In a jumble of movement the horde around the tall man migrated in an unco-ordinated but determined manner towards the designated gate, leaving the man standing alone in the centre of the richly-carpeted passenger lounge. He stooped to pick up the battered suitcase at his feet, braced his shoulders and stepped forwards resolutely, then just as quickly changed his mind and subsided into one of the nearby seats. Setting down the suitcase, he fumbled in the deep pockets of his tweed overcoat, pulling out a wad of papers which he unfolded and studied. The dog-eared state of the papers showed that he had been through this movement many, many times before. The topmost piece of paper was an article cut from a glossy magazine. The tall man stretched open the double sheet and scanned its contents. The article was an in-depth, no-holds-barred, behind-the-scenes feature on the rock band, 'Charlotte Jane'. It had been written by one Dominic Bennett who, according to its accompanying blurb, had succeeded in getting the one interview no other journalist had managed to get purely because he was an old friend of the keyboard player, Avi Livingstone, and the drummer, Kester Simmons.

It was that name, Kester Simmons, in bold, black type that had attracted the attention of the tall man. Surely not! He had stolen the magazine from the library collection. Over the last six months he must have re-read it thousands of times. One day he hoped to thank Dominic Bennett in person. The article was extremely candid. The tall man scanned again the parts that detailed Simmons's long fight against depression, his suicide attempts, his drug addiction and his term in prison.

Parts of the article had been highlighted with an iridescent green pen. The tall man hunted for one of them. Ah! there it was, the name of Simmons's psychiatrist - Dr Margaret Phillips. He turned his attention to the other pieces of paper. Letters, some were copies of his own correspondence and others replies to those letters, the replies topped with Dr Phillips's neat, business-like letterhead. The doctor's answers were equally candid, expanding on Nick Bennett's brief treatise with sordid details that shocked and horrified the tall man, no matter how many times he read them. It was these details that had determined the tall man on his present course of action. He checked another paper, this time a copy of a facsimile message addressed to Michael Kiesanowski. He assumed it had been delivered.

The tall man checked his watch and again braced his shoulders in readiness. No more delays! Time to go. Thrusting the papers back into his pocket, he rose to his feet, snatched up his suitcase and made his way purposefully towards the nearest taxi rank. Thrusting his suitcase before him, he climbed into the nearest vehicle and gave Kit's Avon Loop address to the driver. However, just as soon as he had settled back into the seat, he changed his mind and altered his destination to that of an inner-city hotel. Instead of arriving in a taxi, he would settle in first, have a quiet lunch then walk the short distance to the Loop. It would appear somewhat less formal and he was expecting his arrival to be fraught with quite enough tensions, especially when he confronted Kester Simmons for the first time.

The knot of inquisitive neighbours outside the Avon Loop cottage was depleting. Now that the young owner and his friends had been taken away by police car, there was nothing to watch and the determined constable standing guard at the gate was giving out no information at all. Besides, it was lunch time. Even Nick Bennett had disappeared, scurrying back to his office with the makings of tomorrow morning's front page.

In the workshop John Matheson was still carrying out a fastidious search of the site, using a ball-point pen both in its normal function, taking copious notes, and as a tool for probing, lifting and examining the myriad pieces of seeming junk that littered the room's edges. He talked to himself as he worked, oblivious to the amused sniggers this engendered from the forensic team who had joined him and were by now carrying out their own even more minute search. Matheson paused in his own scrutiny to observe his fellow workers and quickly decided they knew what they were doing and could be left to get on with it while he moved on to more fruitful tasks, or at least while he went into the house to bludge a cup of coffee. He stepped outside, pausing on the doorstep to inhale large lungfuls of fresh air.

The weather was changing, he could feel it. The hot, dry Canterbury nor'wester had a sharper feel to it. Matheson scanned the sky, watching the movement of the rapidly scudding clouds. Yes, the change was coming; by dinner time the nor'wester would give way to a cold southerly. It would probably rain tomorrow. Oh well, that wasn't so bad, maybe he wouldn't have to get up early to take the children to tennis. With a resigned shrug of his shoulders, Matheson headed into the house in search of a drink.

The inside of the cottage took him by surprise. From the look of Simmons he had expected threadbare carpets, dirty, second-hand furniture, empty beer cans and walls full of heavy metal posters. Victoriana? Matheson ran his hand over the back of an exquisitely carved antique dining chair and whistled softly. Polished too. Recently. His eyes went to the mantelpiece. Not a speck of dust. Hmmm!

Trailing his fingers over the counter top, Matheson wandered back into the kitchen. He opened a cupboard, looking for a glass but finding instead a line of small brown bottles, mostly empty. He pulled out the two at the front, unscrewed the lids and tipped the contents out onto the bench. After a minute's thought, he replaced the small white tablets, picked up the bottles and headed back out to the forensic team.

"What do you make of these?" he asked the team's leader who shrugged. "Can we get them analysed?"

"Sure. Leave them with me."

"Soonest?"

"Isn't everything?"

Matheson forgot about his drink.

CHAPTER ELEVEN

Brian Rossiter locked his arms behind his head in a stretch and rocked backwards in his chair. He watched Kit with interest. The young man was scared. Rossiter recognised the signs. Signs, too, of something else. The signs of fear were obvious. Kit shook noticeably, avoided eye contact and had already bitten two fingernails down to the quick. But Rossiter also noticed the signs of a drug user, the continuous body twitching, the dilated pupils. They were having trouble communicating.

"Tell me again, Simmons," Rossiter returned his chair to an upright position. "What happened?"

"I... ah...," Kit ran his hands raggedly through his hair, "I don't know. I've told you. I don't know!"

"Yes. So you have claimed repeatedly. However," Rossiter leaned forwards and rested his arms on the well-worn desk that separated them, "I think we're missing something here. I mean, see my point of view, you live alone, in a tiny little cottage in a nice, quiet neighbourhood where the nights are disturbed only by the gentle quacking of the ducks on the river and you tell me you didn't hear a man being brutally bludgeoned to death in your own backyard. It's a bit far-fetched really, isn't it?"

Kit shrugged.

"I think you must have heard some noise. Something. Anything. So why don't we start again and go over everything from the beginning."

Kit shrugged again and reached shakily for the half-empty packet of cigarettes which lay on the table in front of him.

Rossiter watched carefully as Kit awkwardly fumbled the simple task of extracting a cigarette from the packet and lighting it.

"So when did you last see Daniel Gordon?"

The answer was a long time coming. Kit drew heavily on the cigarette then screwed up his face in thought. Rossiter smiled grimly. He noticed the drummer's body rock with concentration as he tried to get a handle on the question, let alone the answer. This boy was stoned, without a doubt.

"Um...," said Kit finally, "it must have been yesterday afternoon. Yeah, I'm sure it was. Yesterday afternoon."

"What time?"

"Oh, I don't know. Hang on..." Kit thought desperately. "We had a rehearsal. We stopped for lunch then we started again, then Mike's amplifier blew up and we had to stop. Yeah, yeah, Danny left then."

"When did he come back?"

"He didn't."

"Of course he did."

"Not that I knew."

"You must know." Rossiter became insistent. "Did you speak to him? Hear him walk up the drive? See his car parked outside. Come on! Surely you couldn't have missed that?"

Kit shook his head dejectedly.

"I'm sorry. I've told you. I didn't see anything. Look, I don't remember much about the rest of the day. I wasn't feeling well. Please, I still don't feel well, can I go home?"

"Sure. As soon as you've told me the truth."

Avi quoted song lyrics softly to himself in the darkness. It didn't ease the physical pain but it stopped him thinking. Again he went through the laborious exercise of looking at his watch. 12.23. He sobbed aloud.

Elizabeth Livingstone had stopped crying. She had run out of tears. She had cried too many of them for too long. She thought of her son. She remembered the quiet, learned young boy and thought of the sensitive, educated, musical young man he had become. She was proud of him but pride hadn't been enough. Nothing was ever enough for Jacob. Nothing she had ever given him had been good enough. In spite of her best efforts, and the praise of her friends, to him the house was never tidy enough, the food never properly cooked, his trousers never properly pressed, her son never worthy. And only one child. She couldn't even present him with a real family.

Elizabeth Livingstone surveyed her reflection in the bedroom mirror, gently fingering the bruising on her temple. She smiled perversely. He must have been very angry. He didn't even take the time to make sure the bruises were put where they wouldn't show in public. Then quietly, while her husband snoozed in his armchair in the front room, she packed a few belongings into a small bag. Without fuss she carried the bag down the passage and out the back door. From the pocket of her apron she extracted the keys to her son's car. In a flashback of memory, she watched them sail from her son's hand as he reeled under the first blow. She unlocked the boot and placed her bag inside. Then, just as quietly and methodically, piece at a time, she added a bag of clothes for her son, some documents, Avi's electronic keyboard and the housekeeping money. Elizabeth turned the key on the boot, locking her cache safely inside, breathed deeply, returned to her kitchen and served her husband his lunch.

The tall man paused as he rounded the bend to re-adjust his tie and his mindset.

"It's just another deal," he told himself. "It's just another deal."

Confident again, he walked on, only to stop in his tracks at the sight of several policemen, one standing ominously on guard at the front of the neat, white gate, the others shoulder to shoulder, heads down, scouring the riverbank in search formation. The tall man pulled a notebook out of his coat pocket and rechecked the address before approaching the constable on guard.

"What's going on?" he inquired.

"Nothing that need concern you, Sir," the constable answered formally before unbending enough to add, "there's been a homicide."

"What?"

"A young man was found dead, Sir."

"Who?"

"I'm sorry, I'm not at liberty to answer that. I believe it will all be in the paper tomorrow morning."

"The young man who lives here, Kester Simmons. It's not him, is it? He's not dead?"

The constable caught the edge in the tall man's voice. "No, I believe he's at the station, making a statement. Do you have a connection with him?"

The tall man floundered then withdrew a business card from his pocket.

"Barrett, Keith Barrett. I've flown from Wellington especially to see him. A business proposal."

"Sorry, mate. You won't even be able to catch him here later. This place will be roped off for days yet, he won't be able to come back here."

"Damn!" The tall man turned and walked away.

He retraced his steps around the Avon Loop, his head bowed in thought. As he approached the small group of shops he checked his watch. Lunch time. He realised he was hungry, or was that just because of the delicious smells wafting from the little bread shop on the corner. He turned inside. The little man behind the counter began to say something then stopped, words half formed.

"Sorry," he stammered, "I nearly mistook you for someone else. Can I help you?"

Keith Barrett surveyed the arrayed goods and made his choice. The little man continued to chat.

"Nasty business this. Very nasty business."

"What? Bakeries?"

"No. This murder. Haven't you heard about the murder?"

"Yes. Just now."

"Dreadful. 'Charlotte Jane', too. Who would have thought. I know them all, you know. Lovely kids. Shop here regularly, they do."

"It won't do the neighbourhood any good," butted in a woman from behind him. She appeared out from the back of the shop, wiping her hands on a tea towel. "Something like this, it doesn't do the neighbourhood any good at all. It's a nice, quiet neighbourhood we've got around here. I always thought those musicians were a bad influence. I've always said that young man would come to no good. No parents, you know. Father ran off, mother doesn't care. I've always said no good would come of that young man."

"That's hardly fair," remonstrated her husband. "They've always been very polite when they've been in here. Anyway, that horrible supermarket's going to do more damage to the neighbourhood than one young man with a loud set of drums."

As he spoke he wafted his hand vaguely towards a news item, now yellowed by the sun, clipped from a paper and stuck onto the shop window above what appeared to be a petition of some kind. Keith Barrett's eyes were drawn automatically in its direction.

"It'll ruin all of us," the bread shop man continued. "How can we continue our businesses with that thing to compete against?"

Barrett read the article on the proposed supermarket then signed the protest petition in good faith.

"I can sympathise," he said as he paid for his purchases. "I've got a small business myself. Say," he added as an afterthought, "you wouldn't have a phone book I can have a look at, have you? I need to check a couple of addresses."

Brian Rossiter slid into the chair opposite Kit who cowered, dejected and shaking, his cigarette packet empty.

"I'm still waiting for the truth, lad," Rossiter stated quietly.

"I don't know anything," Kit repeated the answer he had given a thousand times.

"Well, I do know some things and I'm pretty sure you're not telling me everything. Shall we start with what I know and see what you can add?"

Kit didn't reply. Rossiter continued.

"To start with, what you've been telling me doesn't add up to what your friends have been telling me. Or should I say you seem to have left out all the important bits."

"What important bits?"

"The on-going fight you and Danny Gordon had been engaged in since Tuesday, for starters. I hear you threw a cup of hot coffee in his face."

"He was being a prick."

"And was he being a prick last night? Is that why you killed him?"

"I didn't kill him, I didn't!"

"But you fought with him. Your friends said so. He tried to fire you. Were you afraid of losing your job? Is that why you killed him?"

"I didn't kill him!" Kit was shouting.

"I think you're lying." Rossiter went very quiet. "We found the murder weapon. In your back yard. Where you threw it. They tell me it's some kind of a chisel, a wood-working tool. It had your initials on the handle. And your fingerprints all over it." Rossiter reached forwards, grabbed Kit's hands and turned them palms up. "What about those?" He indicated several small lacerations on Kit's fingertips. "Did you cut yourself playing the drums? Or struggling with Danny Gordon?"

Kit looked ingenuously at the tiny cuts he hadn't even noticed. He shook more.

Elizabeth Livingstone sat quietly at the neat little kitchen table, her hands folded in her lap, and waited patiently. She looked at the clock on the wall. The time dragged slowly but she had patience. He would leave soon. She could wait. The clock's hands plodded towards 2.30. Finally her husband entered the room, shrugging on his jacket as he walked. They didn't speak. He took his hat from a peg behind the door, placed the hat firmly on his head and strode out the door. As he walked down the driveway, he turned and contemptuously tossed a key into the garden.

Elizabeth watched him go, still without speaking, then, as he stalked off down the street, she rushed forwards to scrabble among the flowers. Snatching up the key she rushed to the little apricot door and desperately worked the key in the padlock. Seconds later she was on her knees beside her injured son.

"Come on!" She choked back a fresh wave of tears brought on by the sight of his swollen face and mangled hand. "Come on, we've got to get out of here."

Gently she helped Avi to his feet, murmuring encouragements when he cried out in agony, half carried him to his car, eased him into the back seat, took her place behind the steering wheel and coaxed the vehicle into life. As she drove away she didn't look back.

The car was temperamental even with a driver who knew it well. Under Elizabeth's inexpert guidance it stalled and bunny-hopped its way through the city streets. By the time she pulled into the emergency entrance of the Christchurch Public Hospital her knuckles were white with tension. In the back seat Avi moaned softly. At the hospital she slung the car into an empty car-park and fled inside in search of help. Soon she returned followed by a strong young man in a white coat, who eased Avi out of the car and into a wheelchair, whipping him rapidly into the sterile realms of the casualty department. As the porter left them in the waiting room, Elizabeth stroked Avi's matted hair.

"It'll be all right now. You're safe now."

Avi reached out his undamaged left hand to squeeze his mother's.

"So are you."

"It's three 'clock."

"Yeah, and all's well. Thanks, Mike."

"That's not what I meant and you know it, Jo."

Jo looked up from the cup of double-strength coffee she cradled in her hands.

"Sorry, Mike. Oh God! I feel so damned useless!"

Kelly reached across the art deco round table and patted her hand.

"Take it easy, Joanna. I think we are all feeling equally shocked and ineffectual. I suggest we compare our individual experiences and rally our collective strength. Would you like another coffee?"

Jo drained her cup hurriedly and held it out to the bass player who had risen from his chair.

"Yes, please. Another double."

"Michael?"

"Thanks, Kelly. White with two."

The remnants of 'Charlotte Jane' had discovered each other in the police station foyer and had wandered, still in a state of shock, to Jo's favourite coffee house in Cashel Mall. Kelly returned to the table, deftly balancing three cups with the skill of a professional waiter.

"White with two, a double and a single," he announced, delivering the cups with a graceful flourish and subsiding into his chair. "So, first, let us go, one at a time, through our respective discussions with the constabulary and see if we can piece together what is happening. Joanna, ladies first."

"I had that policewoman first. She was quite nice. I just told her about us all arriving together this morning; she wanted to know when everyone arrived and in what order. I told her that Danny's car was there when we arrived. She wanted to know why none of us went out to see him earlier, so I had to tell her about the bad mood he had been in for the last few days. Then later that Rossiter chap came in and asked all about the arguments so I sort of had to tell him about Kit throwing the coffee in Danny's face."

"Yeah," broke in Mike. "He asked me about that, too. So I told him it wasn't just Kit who was pissed off with Danny. I admitted punching him out."

"I admitted to the cowardly act of hiding behind the amplifiers," put in Kelly. "You do realise that Kester is the prime suspect in the eyes of the police."

"What makes you think that?"

"I overheard Inspector Rossiter talking in the corridor. Not to mention simple logic. If they considered him innocent, why is he not sitting here with us now?"

"What are we going to do?" Jo asked.

"I think the best thing we could do is seek professional advice. Do you mind if I pull some strings?"

Without waiting for an answer, Kelly thrust his hand into his jacket pocket and pulled out a tiny, black, slimline smart phone, and searched for a number.

"Butler, Finch and Sattherwaite," a female voice answered.

"Yes, good afternoon. Kelly Reynolds for Mr Sattherwaite,

please... Ah, Mr Sattherwaite, Kelly Reynolds speaking. Xavier's son.... Precisely.... I have a small problem..."

After a lengthy conversation in which Kelly said "absolutely" and "certainly" a large number of times, he pocketed the phone and smiled.

"That was an old friend of my father. They were at law school together. He is an excellent criminal lawyer and will meet us back at the police station in about fifteen minutes. He will, thereupon, attempt to extricate Kester as it appears that the police have no right to hold him against his will unless they actually arrest him. Shall we go?"

"Where do you suppose Avi is?" Jo asked as they hurried back to the station.

"That, I think, could turn out to be the six million dollar question," said Mike thoughtfully. "Even if he arrived back just after we'd left Kit's place, you'd think he would have shown up at the station by now."

"Maybe he did," suggested Kelly. "Perhaps we just didn't see him there. We were all in separate rooms. He may have been interviewed in another and allowed to leave."

"Yeah, you're probably right," agreed Mike. "I guess we'll meet up later."

"Hopefully with Kit," added Jo.

Mike stopped suddenly in mid step.

"Okay. I'm going to say it. I feel guilty as hell for thinking it, but I can't help it, and I bet you're both thinking the same thing."

The others turned to face him expectantly.

"What if the police are right. What if Kit did kill Danny." Mike surveyed their expressions. "I'm right, aren't I? You were both thinking the same thing."

Jo and Kelly both nodded.

"Yeah. He has been acting pretty odd,"

"Even for Kit."

"Yesterday, when we were talking about Danny's contract, he said he wanted him dead. It was the calmest I'd heard him talk for two days."

"He does have a flashpoint temper."

"We noticed."

"What if he did kill Danny?"

"We don't tour?"

Keith Barrett crossed the path of the three band members as they left the coffee shop. They failed to notice each other. By the time the trio reached the police station entrance, Keith was already hovering in the foyer, unsure what to do next. He really didn't know what he could do. He knew he should help the young drummer but as he had little idea what was happening, he had even less idea what practical help he could be. Aimlessly, he watched the knot of people enter then stand around, nervously tapping their feet and shuffling. Within a matter of minutes they were joined by a middle-aged, professional-looking man wearing a three-piece dove grey suit and carrying a leather briefcase.

"Lawyer," Keith thought. He was right.

Kelly Reynolds stepped forwards eagerly and acknowledged the newcomer, introducing his companions. The names Reynolds and Greenwood meant nothing to Keith, listening from the corner, but at the mention of Michael Kiesanowski, he began to take notice. That must be the man he had sent the fax to. He looked harder, then withdrew a dog-eared magazine cutting from his coat pocket.

The photograph on the page confirmed it. 'Charlotte Jane'. He listened with intent.

In his clear, Wellington accent, Kelly gave the lawyer a concise report of the day's happenings, adding the fact that Kester appeared to be the prime suspect and listing the altercations of the previous two days that had led them to this conclusion. The lawyer nodded sagely.

"Are you prepared to deal with the possibility that the police may be right? That your young friend may well have killed this Daniel Gordon?"

"Yes" Kelly nodded. "Yes. I guess if we are going to be truly honest, I think we all believe he possibly did."

"If he did, he's going to be in even more need of a good lawyer," put in Mike. "He has a fairly extensive psychiatric history, he may have a reasonable defence."

"Psychiatric history?" questioned the lawyer. "Are you telling me that this boy is in some way challenged?"

"No, not in the way you're thinking. He's quite bright. He's a chronic depressive. The full-nine-yards suicidal bit. And he has been very stressed the last few days."

"Hmm," the lawyer pondered. "Is he likely to be coping with being in there?" He indicated the inner sanctums of the station.

"I doubt it," Mike answered seriously. "He can't even go shopping by himself. And he wasn't coping this morning, even before we got here."

"Then we'd best get him out, hadn't we," the lawyer smiled. "You should all be aware, for your own sakes in this matter, the police cannot hold you if you do not wish to stay."

"I thought they could keep you for up to twenty four

hours, then they had to charge you if they wanted to keep you in any longer," Jo said.

"That, young lady, is a fallacy engendered by too much oversees television. Under New Zealand law the police have no powers to hold you at all. It is all voluntary. You are free to walk out whenever you like. Although I will guarantee that your young friend doesn't know that. However, if you will just remain here, I will go and make further inquiries."

The lawyer made his way towards the desk sergeant, leaving the others in the foyer. Jo gave Kelly a grateful hug.

"Thanks, Kelly. I'll never call you a yuppie again."

Kelly laughed. "Even yuppies have their uses."

"I suppose Kit will qualify for legal aid," Mike mused. "He certainly can't afford a lawyer."

"This affects the whole band. Why don't we pay for it out of tour profits," Jo suggested.

"If there is a tour," Mike reminded her.

"Forget the costs. It can come out of the Reynolds family Christmas liquor budget. God knows, we can afford it," Kelly wrote off their objections.

"I'll help."

The trio turned to see who had spoken. Keith stepped forwards, holding out his hand.

"I'm Keith Barrett. If that is Kester Simmons you are talking about, I'll help."

"You know Kit?" Jo scrutinised the man carefully. He looked familiar but she couldn't place him.

"We haven't met officially. Let's just say I know of him, of you all. If there is a need for funds for legal expenses, I'll help. Here," he fished a business card out of his pocket and thrust it towards Mike. "Any time." He spun on his heel and walked out.

"Who the hell is he?" Mike puzzled.

Jo shrugged. "Who knows. A fan?"

Mike shrugged back.

CHAPTER TWELVE

The lawyer, Sattherwaite, returned to the foyer after what seemed an interminable length of time but which had, in fact, been just over half an hour. Following him, looking shell-shocked, shambled Kit, head bowed. He brightened at the sight of his fellow band members and rushed forwards to be folded into Mike's concerned embrace.

"Are you okay?" Mike asked gently.

Kit looked around wildly.

"Where's Avi?"

"We don't know, mate. We haven't seen him. Let's get you home and worry about Avi later."

"Yeah, take me home."

"If by that you mean Oxford Terrace, Kester, you can't go there, I'm afraid," Sattherwaite interjected.

"Why not?"

"It's a murder inquiry scene, lad. It will be roped off. I'm afraid none of you will get back in there until the police clear the place."

"But..."

"No buts, I'm sorry, son. If there is anything you desperately need, tell me and I will try and clear it with Rossiter. But please don't be silly enough to try and enter the place by yourself, any of you. Is there somewhere else you can stay in the meantime?"

"Yeah," Mike assured. "He can come home with me. In fact, let's all go to my place. It will be a logical place for Avi to find us and I think we should all stay together for a while." He turned to the lawyer. "Thanks for your help, Mr

Sattherwaite. We're very grateful. Here, I'll give you one of my business cards so you know where we are."

Sattherwaite studied the proffered card.

"I'm at your disposal should you need me, Mr..." he stumbled over the pronunciation of the name written before him.

"Kees-an-off-ski," Mike supplied, grinning.

"Mr Kiesanowski," Sattherwaite finished, offering his hand. "Kelly has my number. Good afternoon."

"If we're all going to your place, how are we going to get there? Your car's still at Kit's." asked Jo as the lawyer left.

"Oh," said Mike, who hadn't thought of that. "Hang on." He pulled his cell phone out of his pocket and dialled rapidly.

"Sarah Kiesanowski, please," he began when the call was answered. "It's her husband and, yes, it is urgent." A pause in which he rolled his eyes in mock frustration. "Sarah, Mike. Can you knock off early and collect us? We're at the police station."

"What?" the others heard Sarah's exclamation.

Mike gave his wife a quick explanation of the day's events and she responded with an agreement to collect them, but an apology that she had a client and couldn't be there for at least another half an hour. Mike stole a look at Kit and made a hurried decision.

"We'll start walking. If we go straight through the gardens, we can meet you at the Deans Avenue round-about. Okay?"

"Sure. See you there." She rang off.

"Come on, you lot," he said as he pocketed his phone. "We're hiking. Will you be okay, Kit?"

"Yeah. If it gets me the hell out of here, I'll be fine."

"Then let's move it."

"Can we find a dairy, or something?" Kit asked as they left the station.

"Why? Hungry?" Mike inquired.

"Nah. Need a cigarette." He hunted in his jeans pockets. "Nah, forget it. I haven't got any money, anyway."

"Don't worry, Kit. If you can last until we get home, there's a dairy on the corner. I'll shout you a packet. I hardly think today would be a good day to knock off."

The walk to rendezvous with Sarah took the group through the Botanical Gardens, traversing the same paths Kit and Avi had meandered lazily over only two days before. Only this time Kit was in no mood to appreciate the sights and scents afforded by the carefully tended plots, or the pleasurable expanses of Hagley Park. When they reached the other side of the park they found Sarah waiting for them, posed on the grass with her baby in her arms, like a figure from a Pre-Raphaelite painting. As they approached, she rose, a vision swathed in flowing lilac, and walked towards them. Running ahead of her were two miniature versions of herself, yelling "Daddy, Daddy" and flinging their arms wide. Mike picked his daughters up one at a time, swinging them around giddily. The elder of the two then headed hopefully towards Kit.

"Uncle Kethter, Uncle Kethter, pick me up!"

Kit knelt down to the small child and gave her a hug instead.

"Hi, Chelsea," he said meekly.

The child looked at him sagely.

"You look thick," she announced with finality.

Kit grinned. "Thick or sick?"

"That'th what I thaid, thick!"

"Yeah," Kit agreed, still unsure which way to translate the childspeak. "Right on all counts."

Sarah approached Kit and appraised him with a look similar to that of her child.

"Chelsea's right, Kit. You don't look too good. Are you all right?"

"No," Kit admitted. "No, actually, I feel awful. My throat's dry, my head aches and my balance is a bit fuzzy."

"Then the sooner we get you home, the better. Come on, everyone. Into the car."

"Okay," said Jo, eyeing Sarah's tiny car with dismay. "So who's riding on the roof?"

"Not a problem, not a problem." Sarah extricated one hand from the baby's wrappings and waved it effusively. "Mike, take out the baby seats and throw them into the back."

Mike complied.

"Now," Sarah continued. "It might not be legal but desperation is as desperation does. Mike, you take Rosie and sit in the back. Kit, if you fold those legs of yours around your neck you should just squeeze in. Chelsea can sit on your knee. Jo, could you join them and baby-sit Alice. Kelly, you can sit in the front."

Kelly delivered the others a smugly beatific smirk.

With her charges safely ensconced, Sarah pulled out into the rush-hour traffic.

Avi had lost all sense of time and was now measuring it in hospital cubicles. So the time was now four cubicles past reception. Since their arrival Avi had seen, in order, a male nurse carrying a clipboard who wanted all manner of personal details, which Elizabeth calmly dictated, even patiently spelling Avrahim's name twice, a female nurse who transferred him from the wheelchair onto a trolley then deftly manoeuvred the ungainly contraption down a narrow corridor into the first tiny cubicle, a second male nurse who helped him change from his bloodstained clothes into a crisply clean hospital gown and a female doctor who listened dispassionately to Elizabeth's recounting of her husband's violence, appraised his injuries, which made Avi sob in agony, and, mercifully, authorised a pain-killing injection.

The second male nurse had re-appeared and administered the drug before wheeling the trolley out of the cubicle to deposit it in the hallway with a blithe comment about sending Avi to x-ray. After a very long wait a porter had arrived and soundlessly wheeled the trolley down several corridors to the second cubicle, Elizabeth trailing anxiously behind. There followed another seemingly endless wait until he had been moved again, this time into the x-ray department where his hand and skull were photographed from several angles. It hurt.

Cubicle three had apparently been in the orthopaedic department, where he was sent next. The wait there was so long Elizabeth began to suggest that they had been forgotten when the staff changed shifts. The subsequent visitation from the orthopaedic specialist was much briefer. He spoke of a broken nose, a cracked cheekbone and of multiple fractures to the small bones in the hand. He said Avi would be treated. Then he mentioned concussion and informed them that Avi would be admitted to hospital overnight for observation. It was now the fourth cubicle and Avi was waiting to have his hand, the one he played all the melodies with, encased in a plaster cast.

"Danny is going to kill me when he sees this, Mum."

"There's not much he can do about it, is there. It's not like you did it on purpose, to spite him."

"Mum, you don't know Danny. To hear him talk, creation was designed to spite him."

"Well, you don't have to take him so personally."

"True. Look, Mum, if they're going to make me stay here all night, I'd better let the band know. They'll either be steaming mad or beside themselves with worry already and if I walk in tomorrow with no warning and a plaster cast, I'm dead meat. Once we find out what ward I'm going to be in, would you mind ringing Kit to tell him what's happened?"

"Should I guess? Will he be steaming mad or beside himself with worry?"

Avi attempted to grin through the bruises.

"What do you think?"

The television news was mercifully scanty. A reporter on the scene spoke in hushed, over-dramatic tones about the grisly discovery of a body in the back shed of a house in an inner-city Christchurch suburb. The camera panned back to show the front of Kit's house, wisteria in full bloom, while the voice-over advised clinically that no details of the deceased were being released as the next of kin had not yet been notified. Kit sighed with relief.

Throughout dinner the topic of Danny's murder had been judiciously avoided but now that the children were safely tucked up in bed the conversation was taking a harder edge. Kit had haltingly recalled his discussions with Rossiter and staunchly maintained his lack of knowledge. The others, in their turn, told their own tales, first Jo then Kelly and lastly Mike.

"By the way," Mike added. "Who the hell is Keith Barrett?"

"Keith Barrett?" Kit repeated.

"Yeah. A guy about your height, late forties, grey hair, very square hands. Hang on." Mike rummaged in his pocket and pulled out a handful of business cards. "Yeah, here." he handed Barrett's card to Kit. "This Keith Barrett,"

"Oh, No! That Keith Barrett. Damn! I'd forgotten all about him." Kit looked at the others. "He was coming to meet me today. All the way from Wellington."

"I get it," Mike exclaimed with a flash of inspiration. "K.B. Keith Barrett. That's who sent that James Bond fax."

"Yeah," Kit explained. "And probably the phone call that Kelly took. He's offered me a business deal. I'm going to take him up on it because I need the money, but just between you guys, I'm not sure if it's strictly honest."

"That sounds ominous, Kit," broke in Sarah. "Are you sure you should be doing... whatever it is you're going to do?"

"No," Kit shook his head. "I'm not sure at all but, like I said, I need the money. You other guys, you've all got real jobs apart from the band. Well, Kelly hasn't but he obviously doesn't need one. But I rely on fixing bits of furniture and I'm slowly starving to death on that. I know Mum and Gabriel reckon I'm not fit to do anything much but Dr Phillips put this guy onto me, so she must think it's okay."

"So what's the job?" Jo asked, all attention.

"Oh, sorry, um... making furniture. You know, like the stuff I've got at home. Stuff that looks like it's real old. That's the catch. This guy Barrett has an antique shop in Wellington. I reckon he's going to sell my replicas as the real thing and that's not legal."

"Then don't do it."

"Nice morals, Jo, but like I said, I'm seriously broke and seriously desperate. Look, I've only told Avi this but.. well, you know I said I didn't have any money for cigarettes before? Yeah, well I haven't had any money for four days. One of the reasons I was drumming so badly the other day was because I couldn't afford to buy any food."

"Kit, that's dreadful!" Sarah was full of concern. "You should have said something."

"I did. I told Avi."

"When do you get paid next?" Mike inquired.

"Not till next week."

"And you've got no money at all."

"No."

"This happens regularly?"

"Yeah."

"Well, don't worry about it," Sarah took charge. "On Monday we'll take you in to the Social Welfare and see about an emergency grant. Do you know how much you usually get?"

"Not really. Mum and Gabriel handle all my money for me because they reckon I'll only stuff it up. Gabriel's been giving me fifty dollars, but it doesn't go very far."

"Fifty dollars? To live on? Do you have a lot of debts then? Is that where the rest of your money's going?"

"No. None, oh, except the usual power and phone."

"Mortgage?"

"No."

"Then you're being ripped off, Kit. I think we need to have a word with your brother."

"That's what Avi said."

"Speaking of Gabriel," cut in Mike, "Kit, Gabriel brought you some medication yesterday. I know you're supposed to take it regularly. Have you got it with you?"

"Hell! No,... no I haven't."

"Leave that to me," said Sarah, unfolding herself from the couch. "I'll call Margaret Phillips. I think she should know what's happening anyway, especially if the police continue to hassle Kit." She hurried off to the telephone.

Brian Rossiter polished his glasses feverishly in frustration.

"Damn it, John!" He pounded his fist into the desk between himself and Senior Sergeant John Matheson. "That boy is as guilty as hell. I know he did it. His fingerprints are all over the murder weapon. He's even got fresh cuts on his fingers."

"That won't hold up in court and you know it," Matheson answered. "He's a qualified tradesman. He uses that thing. If the murderer wore gloves, of course Simmons's prints will be the only ones on it. However, take a look at this, it might interest you."

Matheson held out a computer printout. Rossiter scanned it and shrugged.

"Explain!"

"I found a couple of pill bottles in Simmons's kitchen cupboard. I gave them to the forensic people. That's the analysis. Quite interesting really, especially from what you say of Simmons's past form. Most of the tablets are pretty innocuous. Something called lithium carbamazepine.

According to this note it's standard long-term medication for chronic depression. Simmons must be a pretty sick young man."

"So I gather."

"But this is where it gets interesting. The chemist who did this analysis noticed that two of the tablets were slightly grainier, so he checked them separately."

"Okay, hit me with it. What 's in them?"

"Good old-fashioned L.S.D."

Rossiter rubbed his hands with glee.

"Good work, John! I knew there was something. I was sure that lad was off his face when he was in here this morning. So much for all that crap about reforming. He's still the same pathetic junkie he always was."

He rose from his chair and stretched languidly.

"I'll guarantee you, John, that if we keep digging through this little muck heap we'll find drugs at the bottom. Especially where Kester Joseph Simmons is concerned."

'Charlotte Jane' was nearly water-logged with coffee. Sarah held out a fresh cup to Jo who re-entered the immaculate cream-upholstered lounge, rubbing her ear.

"Well, he's still not answering his cell phone and I've tried everywhere else I can think of," she said ruefully. "I got extremely short shrift from Uncle Jacob. I asked him if Avi was at home and he just bellowed 'No' and slammed the phone down in my ear. I rang our place. Mum had conniptions when I told her Danny had been killed but she hasn't heard from or about Avi all day. I tried the music department at the university. I couldn't figure why he'd go there with all this going on, but it was a long shot. Anyway, he wasn't there. The coffee shop hasn't seen him and there's no answer at your place, Kit, surprise, surprise. So, I'm afraid, no Avi."

"Maybe his car has broken down," Mike suggested. "It's about the only possibility left."

"So why didn't he phone one of us?" Kit asked.

"Maybe he tried. We have been kind of pre-occupied today."

"Get real, Mike. We can still hear our phones. We've been here for hours now. He should have called or at least sent a text."

"I hate to say it," Jo said quietly. "Kit's right. Even if he was on foot he would have got here by now. If nothing else, if I know my cousin as well as I think I do, he would have phoned out of sheer guilt for missing today's rehearsal."

"So where is he?" Kit was beginning to sound genuinely worried.

Jo drained her coffee. "Okay, it's my turn to jump to conclusions. I don't want to be a scaremonger but I can't stop thinking something awful might have happened to him."

"Like what?"

"Like we don't know who the hell killed Danny last night. Maybe they got Avi as well. Maybe he's a hostage or something."

"Maybe he's dead," added Kelly.

"Hang on a bit," enjoined Mike. "Let's not assume anything so drastic. Hey," he paused at the sound of the doorbell. "That's probably him now."

Mike leapt up to answer the door. Standing outside was a well dressed middle-aged woman, her greying hair pulled back into a serviceable bun, her face alive with a wide smile and twinkling green eyes.

"Hi, Doctor Phillips, come on in."

"Hello, Michael. Sarah asked me to call and check on Kit. I believe you've all had a rough day."

"Yeah," agreed Mike, ushering Margaret Phillips through the passage and into the lounge. Kit favoured her with a wan smile.

"Kit," she began, settling into a kneeling position on the floor beside his chair. "Sarah rang me. I've brought you over some more tablets. Sarah said that you can't get back to your house, so I made the prescription out for a month. I don't think you'll need anything like that amount but it's best to be safe, isn't it."

She handed Kit two bottles.

"This one is the lithium. Those are the ones you take every day. This other bottle is the chlorpromazine. Now look carefully. I've written my phone number on the bottle. If you feel really bad and you need help, phone me straight away, then take one of these. Promise? I know young Avrahim has a supply of these, but I want you to carry this bottle in your pocket all the time. Especially if you have to go back to the police station. Promise?"

Kit nodded.

"I promise. You haven't heard from Avi, have you?"

"No, should I have?"

"He's on the missing list," Jo cut in. "Nobody's seen him all day. He said he was planning to stay at Kit's last night, but he wasn't there when we got there this morning and he hasn't turned up anywhere since. To be perfectly honest we were just beginning to wonder if the murderer got him as well."

"Stop saying that!" Kit shouted at her.

Margaret Phillips put a comforting arm around his bony shoulders and threw Jo a warning glare.

"Did Avi stay with you last night?" she asked Kit gently.

"Yeah, I think so, yeah, I'm sure he did."

"You don't sound terribly sure."

Kit wrung his hands nervously.

"I don't remember much about last night. I've been feeling really strange for the last few days."

Margaret was suddenly all attention.

"What sort of strange, Kit. Can you describe it?"

"If it was a drum beat I would say my snare is a sixteenth behind the hi-hats. Everything's vaguely out of sync. And all those weird symptoms I told you about last time I saw you have got worse. And last night was truly ghastly. I think if the others are honest they will say that I was acting pretty weird. Avi gave me one of those chlor-whatever tablets at lunch time. I think it was the second one in two days..."

Margaret raised her eyebrows.

"Anyway," Kit continued, "I had these weird dreams all night. I kept seeing these huge, hairy spiders with red hair. They were trying to eat me. I can remember them walking up and down the driveway, yelling at each other. No! Wait a minute! Maybe it wasn't all dream. When the spiders were yelling, one of them sounded like Avi."

"So who was the other one?"

"Danny. I'm sure it was Danny."

Margaret paraphrased. "So you heard people in your driveway, but you thought they were spiders?"

"No, I heard spiders, but they might have been people."

"Okay. One of the spiders might have been Avi?"

"Yeah."

"And the other might have been Danny?"

"Yeah."

"When did you last see Avi?"

Kit thought carefully. "This morning. He brought me breakfast and said he was going home to have a shower."

"Why?" asked Jo.

"Why what?"

"Why go home for a shower. You've got one at your place."

"Yeah, but he wanted some clean clothes as well."

"Fair enough."

"There were extra breakfast dishes in the sink," Mike agreed.

"So Avi was at your place this morning, left before you others arrived and hasn't been seen since?" Margaret was still paraphrasing the information.

"Pretty much," Kit acknowledged.

"Did he mention Danny this morning?"

"No."

"Did you see Danny this morning?"

"No. Avi woke me and told me he was leaving. I don't even remember him going. I was barely awake and I must have gone straight back to sleep."

"He was pretty wasted still, even when we got there," Mike filled in. "We had to haul him out bodily and throw him under the shower. We found Danny just after that."

"You do realise there is another logical scenario here?" Kelly interjected. The others stared at him. "Maybe it's Avrahim the police should be questioning, not Kester."

"What are you getting at?" Kit demanded savagely.

Kelly leant back lazily, clasped his hands behind his head

and spoke slowly. "Avrahim is heard in the driveway yelling at Daniel, Daniel is found dead and Avrahim has decamped from the scene. Personally, I would consider such decampment highly suspicious."

"You're not serious?" Jo was incredulous. "Avi. Murder Danny. Get real, Kelly."

"Why not?"

"Because he's Mister Nice Guy, that's why not. He's so nice he's nauseous."

"I think Jo's right, Kelly," Mike agreed. "I can't imagine Avi getting angry enough, even with Danny, to kill him."

"I can," Kit said softly. "I've only ever seen him angry twice, but both times he beat the crap out of guys a lot bigger than himself."

"Do you think we should tell the police that he's missing?" Sarah suggested.

"Tomorrow." Mike wasn't prepared to believe the worst yet. "We'll give him until tomorrow."

"Kit," Margaret Phillips changed the topic. "I have someone in the car I want you to meet. But only if you think you can handle it. Are you feeling okay?"

"Yeah. Who?"

"I'll go and get him. He can introduce himself."

As the psychiatrist made her way out the front door, Jo pulled Kelly roughly into the kitchen and hissed in his ear.

"You're so keen on scenarios, try this one. How about Mike as the bad guy."

"Michael! Don't be ridiculous," Kelly whispered back.

"It's no more ridiculous than your suggestion that it was Avi," Jo retorted. "And I might have evidence."

"What?"

"Tuesday, after Mike had hit Danny in the face, Mike gave me a lift into town. When I left him he said something about hiring a hitman to cancel Danny's contract permanently. Then he told me not to tell anyone, not even to say that he'd given me a lift. And after all," she finished righteously, "Mike was pretty quick to get us thinking Kit was guilty."

"Oh, come now! We are all thinking that. He was just the first to say it."

Jo's reply was halted by Dr Phillips who returned accompanied by a man who stepped forwards and shook Mike's hand.

"Hi there," he said in an accent with American overtones. "We meet again."

"You're Keith Barrett," exclaimed Jo.

"Yes and no," replied the newcomer.

"Look, at the risk of being rude, which I'm accused of frequently, who are you? You look familiar but I'm sure I've never met you before."

"That's quite all right, young lady," the man replied "You haven't met me, at least not before today, but I can understand why I seem familiar. It's called family resemblance. My business card says Keith Barrett, but that's only half of it. Barrett's really my middle name. I haven't used my real surname for about twenty years. I'm Keith Simmons. I'm Kester's father."

Kit stared at him blankly.

CHAPTER THIRTEEN

The silence was tangible. Kit sat back in the couch and eyed his father evenly.

"Then why the lies?"

No-one spoke.

"Why didn't you say who you were from the beginning? Why go through all that crap about a furniture deal? Why pretend to be someone else?"

Keith gave a snort of self-derision. He moved to sit beside his son.

"Um...," He bowed his head to the side and looked up with the same spaniel-like expression the others had come to expect from Kit. "I was nervous. It's been a long time. I had no idea what you might think of me, whether you would even talk to me. The furniture deal's genuine, I assure you. My partner and I really do have a shop in Wellington. I wanted to tell you straight off who I was but I thought that you would either tell me to go to hell, or you would think that the deal was made out of charity and refuse it. I assure you it isn't."

"So instead of thinking it's charity, I think it's shonky," Kit laughed. "Terrific!"

"Shonky? Why did you think that?"

"Some American guy I've never heard of asks me to make furniture that looks like antiques. I thought you were planning to sell replicas as real antiques and were getting me to make them because I was too broke and too crazy to complain."

"If your name's really Simmons," broke in Jo, "how come

your business cards say Barrett? Surely you didn't have them specially printed just to impress Kit?"

"No," Keith flashed her a wide smile. "I haven't used Simmons for twenty three years. Not since I left New Zealand."

"Why did you leave?" Kit asked directly. "Was I that much of a disappointment?"

Keith reached forwards tentatively to touch his son.

"Don't ever think that. On the contrary, I was inordinately proud of you. My only son. It was the situation that became intolerable. It had nothing to do with you."

"I'm not your only son. Remember Gabriel?"

Keith took a deep breath before explaining.

"Gabriel isn't mine. I met your mother at university. She was a first year, reading classics. I was in my final year of a maths degree, heading for a career as a teacher. We met through a flatmate of mine. Believe it or not, we never dated. Looking back, I'm not even sure if we ever really even liked each other." He looked at Kit's puzzled expression.

"It was a marriage of convenience," he continued. "Catherine had an affair with a junior lecturer and found herself pregnant. He didn't want to know, hadn't bothered to tell her about the wife and kid he already had and wasn't about to throw away a promising career for a daffy fresher. So she was pregnant and desperate. And I guess I was desperate in my own way." He turned to Margaret Phillips beseechingly and received a nod of approval in return.

"I had been aware for some time that I was gay. But, please remember, this was over twenty years ago, things were different. I wanted to be a teacher. It's probably hard enough now to teach if you're gay, it was impossible then. I needed some respectability. Catherine offered it. We got married, It was a disaster from the start and after Gabriel was born it got progressively worse. We toughed it out because in those days you didn't get divorced very easily. At times we even tried to make it work. It was in one of those times that you were conceived, Kester. I thought you were fantastic from the moment you were born. You looked like me, even as a baby. You were all black hair and long legs. Not like Gabriel. He was so like his mother."

"He still is," Kit supplied. "What made you leave?"

"Bobby. You were about six months old and the marriage had become a battleground. Catherine screamed and yelled and threw things and I didn't speak at all. I spent most of my time out at the jazz club. That's where I met Bobby. I was playing saxophone in a five-piece and he joined us one night on trumpet. A month later I chucked in my job and we lit out. We've spent the last twenty three years playing jazz in New Orleans."

"Choice!" Jo's admiration was unfeigned.

"We came back to New Zealand last year," Keith finished. "I've been planning this meeting since then."

Brian Rossiter was searching for drugs. Or, more specifically, evidence that Simmons had been up to his old tricks - selling drugs. He was sure he would find it, even if he had to turn the whole house upside down. The young constable at the gate had been surprised to see him.

"Working late, Sir," he had inquired cheerfully.

"No rest for the wicked," Rossiter had replied.

He had let himself into the cottage with a set of duplicate keys that had been supplied by an obliging locksmith earlier in the day. As he had switched on the lights he had shared John Matheson's earlier surprise at the place's pristine neatness. Barely a thing out of place. At least, there hadn't been when he had started searching.

Now in the bedroom the contents of the drawers had been tipped out into a huge pile on the floor, the drawers themselves dumped unceremoniously in a heap in one corner. The meagre contents of the wardrobe had quickly heightened the pile after each had been subjected to a pocket by pocket search.

Rossiter's attention had then moved to the lounge. His own love of fine china had forestalled a similarly irreverent hunt but he had been no less thorough. So far it had been a fruitless exercise. A likely looking pile of correspondence contained nothing but catalogues and order forms from mail order modelling supply shops. A cryptic note scrawled on the edge of an old envelope proved to be nothing more than a reference to Israeli army tank markings and the only available evidence of substance abuse was a used tube of plastic glue. Rossiter was frustrated. He moved to the fireplace to light himself a cigarette. As he bent to discard the used match, he paused, his attention riveted on an article that lay on the hearth.

"What the hell...?"

He knelt, carefully picking up the mutilated photograph. A brief search located the photo's missing piece, still impaled on the mantelpiece by a modelling knife. Rossiter pondered. Was the photo cut and left as a warning to Simmons? Or was the boy inflicting some sort of self-mutilation-by-proxy? It was another piece to the ever-widening jigsaw.

Rossiter straightened, drawing deeply on his cigarette.

His eyes scanned the room. Somewhere he would find the answer. But where? It was all so neat. But there must be a clue somewhere. His gaze fell on the piece of paper that lay, out of place amongst the neatness, dropped casually on the kitchen bench. He rushed to pick it up, his face breaking into a wide smile as he read its contents.

"Gotcha!" he exclaimed gleefully as he folded the fax into his pocket.

From the safety of the Barbadoes Street cemetery, Cassandra Oakleigh watched the policeman come and go. She knew what was happening. Finding out had been easy. After her precious Kit had been led away earlier in the day, she had simply strolled across and joined in the groups of spectators who had clustered around, aimlessly watching the action. The man at the bread shop had been a mine of information. Mind you, he always was. She got a lot of her information on the band from the man at the bread shop. They told him and he told her. Simple.

She wrapped her denim jacket tighter around her body. It was cold in the cemetery at night but she had become accustomed to it long ago. By now she knew exactly which way the wind blew and exactly which headstones offered protection from it without obscuring her view of the little house across the river. Cassandra watched the policeman leave. She could go over soon and have a look around herself. Maybe she could tidy up a bit. Make it nice for Kester when he got home again. He'd like that.

Keith Barrett-Simmons reached gratefully for the coffee Sarah had provided.

"Like I said, Kester," he said in an effort to reaffirm his motivation. "I did my best."

"Yeah, sure." Kit was not prepared to let his father off the hook that easily. "Leaving me with a mother who hated me and 'litting out', as you put it, was doing your best."

"Believe me, it didn't come easy. At first I tried to take you with me. I got a lawyer to fight for custody but, like I said, this was twenty three years ago. Courts just didn't give custody to fathers. It was considered the proper thing to do to leave the child with its mother, no matter what the circumstances. Even the best father in the world had little chance. There was no way the courts would give a baby to a gay saxophone player with a boyfriend in tow."

"I guess not," Kit conceded grudgingly.

"I had swags of legal advice, I'll show you the files one day. In the end they convinced me to let things lie. I believed them. I see now that it was a wrong decision, but I'm very good at taking steps for what seems all the right reasons, only to discover later that I've stuffed up markedly."

"Do I get that from you. Mum said I was just naturally stupid."

"I suspect you are far too like me. That may well be the cause of your mother's dislike. She despised me before I left and loathed me afterwards. I guess she took it out on you. And all I could do was throw money."

Kit knitted his brow.

"To Mum?"

"Yes, by court order. But I knew you'd see precious little of that, so I fed another lot to you, by way of my parents. Dad said he was going to save it for your education."

Kit laughed openly.

"He did, in a strange sort of a way. My education went down the tubes in the fourth form. My education fund went to buy drum lessons and then my drums. I always wondered where Granddad got that sort of money, especially after buying me the van when he stopped driving." He stopped suddenly as the memory of the day's events washed back. "Oh, God, my drums. They're slashed to pieces!"

Keith sought to steer the conversation in another direction.

"Don't worry. Better the drums than you. Drums can be fixed. Tell me more about yourself. Margaret tells me you have a very caring partner, a young lad from your band. Am I going to get an introduction?" He looked inquiringly in Kelly's direction.

"Don't look at me," Kelly laughed, rising and coming forwards to shake Keith's hand. "I'm Kelly and I'm straight."

In a rush of embarrassment, Kit effected overdue introductions and then added,

"Avi's missing. He left my place this morning, before I was awake, and he hasn't been seen since. We were talking about it when you arrived." He neglected to explain that their relationship was not as close as his father had suggested.

"In fact," Kelly added, "We were discussing the likelihood of Avrahim being either a second victim, or the perpetrator of the crime."

"Kelly!" Jo and Sarah exclaimed together.

"For heaven's sake, Kelly!" Jo continued. "Haven't you got a grain of tact? Can't you see Kit is worried enough?"

Rossiter studied the exterior of the Riccarton property. He checked through a pile of notes on his lap. The statement said Michael Vivian Stanislaus Kiesanowski. Rossiter squinted through the gloom of the street light at a discreet sign affixed to the front fence. 'Key Engineering Consultancy. M.V.S. Kiesanowski M.E.' Must be the right place. He studied the house again. Obviously the Kiesanowskis were not broke. It was a good area and theirs was an expensive-looking dwelling; permanent materials, cream summerhill stone under a tile roof, wrought iron gates across a slate-paved driveway.

"I bet there's a pool and a barbeque out the back," Rossiter thought wryly. He would have won the bet. There was.

Stuffing the notes back into a cardboard folder, Rossiter unfolded himself from his car and locked it behind him. Adjusting his tie, he made his way to the front door and rang the bell. It was answered in short order by Mike who looked anything but pleased at the policeman's presence.

"What do you want?" he demanded.

"I want to talk to Simmons. May I come in?"

Mike hesitated then grudgingly instructed him to follow. Rossiter trailed after Mike to where the others were seated. Kit stiffened at the policeman's arrival.

"What the hell does he want?" The question was directed to Mike.

"He wants to talk to you," Mike supplied.

"Well I don't want to talk to him."

"I have a couple more questions, Simmons," Rossiter tried the calm approach. "It won't take long."

"I don't care. I'm not answering anything."

"We can talk here or we can talk at the station, take your pick."

"Go to hell! I don't have to talk to you at all. The lawyer said so. You can't make me. Go to hell!"

"Maybe it would be better to answer his questions," Keith suggested. "If you're not guilty, you've got nothing to worry about. Surely you want them to catch whoever killed Danny?"

"I don't care who killed Danny!" Kit was shouting. "And I don't care if they never catch him. Good on him. Danny got what he deserved. I'm glad he's dead. And I'm not talking to you. Go to hell!"

Rossiter shrugged.

"This is not a good attitude, Simmons," he persisted.

"Forget it," Mike ushered him towards the door. "He's right. Sattherwaite said we don't have to talk to you so if Kit says no, unless you've got a warrant for his arrest, you'll just have to leave. Good night, Inspector."

Rossiter went reluctantly.

"You can take that attitude if you like, Simmons," he called back over his shoulder, "but I can wait. I'll be back."

"I just want to go home," Kit sighed as the policeman departed.

"I don't blame you," Keith again tried to lighten the atmosphere. "You've kept the place very nicely."

"You've been there?"

"Yes. I went there this morning, expecting to hold a business meeting about furniture, remember? I didn't get inside. I was turned away by the police at the gate. But I did think it looked just the way Mum had it."

"I've tried to keep it that way, yeah," Kit admitted. "It's a lot of work, though, all that garden."

"You'll be glad to sell off the back then."

"No way! I'm not selling any of it."

Keith looked abashed at his son's determined answer.

"Sorry, I must have it wrong. I stopped at a little bakery near your place. The little man behind the counter was raving on about some supermarket that was going up in the area. He conned me into signing a petition to protest against it. The article with the petition said all the properties needed for it had been sold and I thought the map covered the back of your place. So I figured you must be sub-dividing."

"No way!" Kit repeated. "They offered, several times. I told them where to stick it. If you'd looked carefully you would see my signature right at the top of the petition."

"Okay, okay," Keith spread his hands in a placatory gesture. "I'm sorry I spoke. I'm glad you feel that way though. It's a lovely old house. I don't suppose that old tree house is still down the back?"

"No, Granddad cut the tree down about nine years ago." Kit looked shamefaced. "I tried to hang myself from it."

Cassandra Oakleigh ducked down behind the tree stump and waited. It had been harder than usual to get onto Kester's property. She couldn't just slide quietly down the drive as she normally did. It had instead meant taking a tortuous route over several back fences. Now she was in she hid for while, to make sure she hadn't been spotted as well as to catch her breath. She waited, eyes darting, body alert. When nothing challenged her presence she made a cautious move forwards. A twig snapped beneath her Doc Martin boot. Ahead of her a small figure darted out from between rows of vegetables. Cassandra jumped, a cry of alarm frozen on her lips. The cat glared at her balefully. She giggled with relief.

Another few strides took her safely to the rear of the laundry where she deftly removed the louvres from the small window and hauled herself inside. She pulled a small penlight torch out of her pocket, shielding it with her hand to keep the light from showing out the front windows as she carefully edged her way through the darkened house. She could smell the policeman's distinctive tobacco.

The sight of the bedroom made her gasp. Kester would be horrified. She knelt reverently on the floor by the pile of clothing. She would make it right. After all, she knew where everything went. She knew as well as Kester. It may take her several hours, especially in the dark, but she would make it right. Cassandra reached forwards, picked up a t-shirt from the top of the pile and held it close to her face. His scent filled her nostrils. She breathed it in, her eyes closing, her lips parting in sensuous pleasure. Humming one of the band's more romantic tunes to herself, she set to work.

Elizabeth Livingstone tucked herself up in the middle of the large motel bed and revelled in the luxury. A whole bed, all to herself. It was a long time since she had last indulged in that privilege. She sipped daintily at her cup of tea and smiled. The nurses had been so kind and the lady from the women's refuge had been so willing to help. She had tried to insist that Elizabeth go with her for the night but there had been no need for that. Elizabeth was capable of handling things herself, her own way. It was time she took control. Anyway, the motel was so nice.

She thought of her son, alone in a much starker bed in Christchurch hospital. She had offered to stay but he had declined her offer. He was quite right, of course. He wasn't a baby any more and there was little point in her sitting uncomfortably at his bedside. They would both get a good night's sleep this way.

She thought of her husband. By now he would have realised that neither of them were coming home. He would be furious. And hungry. It was now well into the Sabbath. He wouldn't have cooked for himself earlier in the evening, expecting her to return. He couldn't do it now. She felt no guilt.

In a fit of perverse rule-breaking, Elizabeth turned on the television. It was thirty years since she had seen television on a Friday night. The movie was boring. Gently she drifted off to sleep. When the late news covered the story of the day's murder, she didn't see it.

Brian Rossiter had polished his glasses so hard one of the lenses had fallen out. This did not improve his temper. He glared at the paper John Matheson was holding out to him.

"This had better contain something I can use," he muttered darkly.

"Oh, I think it might," the detective sergeant gave him a benign smile. "It's the autopsy report on Daniel Gordon."

"Already? That was quick."

"Well, it wasn't all that complicated. Death inflicted by a stab wound from a sharp instrument which, as we already know, was a narrow-bladed chisel. There were five lesser wounds as well as the one which obviously caused the death, so we can surmise the attacker made several attempts before the blade sank deep enough to hit anything vital. Gordon appears to have been very well developed muscularly, so that isn't too surprising. There are the usual signs of a struggle -

cuts to his forehead and lip."

"Those could have come from the earlier punch-ups between Gordon and Kiesanowski and Simmons," Rossiter pointed out.

"True," Matheson admitted. "The report does note that some of the minor injuries were more than twenty four hours old."

"So far there's nothing we didn't already know."

"I told you it was fairly straightforward. The only interesting thing were his muscles."

"I didn't realise you were that way inclined," Rossiter grinned.

"Do you want to hear this or not? Daniel Gordon was extremely well developed. The sort of muscles you only get from spending a lot of time in a gym. Consequently, I wasn't all that surprised to find the blood analysis showing large traces of anabolic steroids. On top of that he was showing a couple of other classic signs of steroid abuse, some kidney damage and, just to offset the macho muscles, shrunken testes."

"Steroids, eh? Now that is interesting. Let me run something by you. We have a murdered man, chock full of steroids, found in the house of a known junkie with a record for dealing. Said junkie was high as a kite when we brought him in. We find L.S.D. tablets in the junkie's kitchen and I find this on the kitchen bench." Rossiter removed the folded fax from his pocket and passed it across the desk to his associate.

Matheson read the fax without comment.

"Add to that," Rossiter continued, "the fact that it is our junkie's fingerprints all over the murder weapon and that he seems mighty unwilling to talk to us. Am I wrong in suspecting a connection?"

"I would certainly lean in that direction," Matheson agreed.

"So I take it you will have no objections to accompanying me tomorrow morning. I intend to have a further chat with Kester Joseph Simmons, whether he wants to co-operate or not!"

Sarah woke up with a start. Mike stirred beside her.

"Are you okay?"

"Oh Mike, I didn't mean to wake you. I had a vision."

Mike sat up. He had grown used to his wife's psychic abilities and knew not to question them.

"What? What did you see?"

"Little cells. Rows of little cells. First I was in a dark one. Pitch black. Then I was moved, like I was on some kind of conveyor belt, through lots of bright ones. And there was such pain. I can still feel that. In my right hand. Dreadful pain."

CHAPTER FOURTEEN

Sarah surveyed the sleeping forms of the three extra band members strewn at odd angles across her lounge. Margaret Phillips had left just after eleven o'clock the previous night, accompanied by Kit's newly rediscovered father, whom she had promised to deliver back to his inner-city hotel.

Kit had stayed. He had nowhere else to go. Jo and Kelly had opted to stay as well, sacrificing their own more comfortable sleeping arrangements in favour of the general need to stay together. Solidarity in numbers. Jo had pulled two armchairs together to form a temporary bed and Kelly had purloined the couch. Kit, too long in the leg for either option, was curled up on a foam camping squab in the middle of the floor.

Mike was attempting to make coffee in the kitchen, as quietly as possible. That was the one disadvantage of open-plan house designs. Still, it didn't happen very often. He held up a mug and pointed at it with his spare hand to indicate that coffee was made and Sarah tip-toed out to join him.

"Sleeping like babies," she whispered.

"I hope our baby stays asleep a little while longer," Mike whispered back. He glanced at the clock on the electric range. "I hope she sleeps until at least half past six. What the...?"

He put his mug down hurriedly as the second thump crashed against the front door. Down the hall a child cried out. Mike flung open the door to find himself confronted by Brian Rossiter, John Matheson and two uniformed constables. A white car with its distinctive blue stripe ticked in the driveway.

"For God's sake!" Mike expostulated angrily. "It's six o'clock in the bloody morning. What do you want?"

"I want to speak to Kester Simmons." Rossiter hoped his tone would allow no arguments.

"He told you last night that he didn't want to talk to you. What makes you think he's going to want to now?"

"Then the least he can do is tell me that himself."

"I'll see."

Mike turned, intending to call Kit. Rossiter used the movement to put his foot over the doorstep.

"Hold it right there!" Mike ordered, swinging back to face the policeman and placing a restraining hand on Rossiter's chest. "I haven't invited you in and I don't intend to. Not unless Kit is willing to talk."

"No!" Kit's lanky form loomed into the passage behind Mike. "I told you yesterday, go to hell!"

"Come now," Rossiter reasoned. "Can't we talk this over calmly. I just have a couple of questions. If Simmons will supply the answers we will leave you in peace. Can we come in? I'm sure you don't want all this broadcast to the neighbours."

"I don't give a toss about the neighbours," Kit muttered belligerently. Mike grinned.

"Okay, have it your own way," Rossiter shrugged. "We'll stand out here. Tell me about drugs."

"I don't do drugs any more. You know that."

"I know that, do I? Wrong, Simmons. What I know is that your friend Gordon was using them and we found two tablets of L.S.D. in your kitchen. So let's try again. Tell me about drugs."

"Go to hell!"

Kit turned away but hadn't made more than two paces when the uniformed constables pushed their way past Mike. They grabbed an arm each and slammed Kit up against the passage wall. Rossiter stepped forwards and calmly slapped on a set of plastic handcuffs.

"I came here to talk, Simmons, but if you want to be difficult, I'll play your silly game. You're under arrest."

"What for?" Mike interjected.

"Possession of L.S.D. for a start. And the murder of Daniel Gordon. Get him out of here."

Kit fought back wildly as the two constables tried to lead him to the car but ultimately he could not withstand their combined pressure and he was bundled into the back seat. Mike heard him screaming for help as they drove away.

Kit's mind was beginning to play tricks on him. The ordeal of processing had been every bit as harrowing as it had been the last time. Familiarity, in Kit's case, had not bred contempt so much as heightened terror - each step leading him more certainly towards his greatest nightmare.

The two constables had dragged him forcibly into the Central Police Station through the back entrance, the one reserved for criminals, and had hauled and pushed him through the various requirements of search, fingerprinting and identity photograph. The search had revealed only a handkerchief, an empty cigarette packet and a bottle of pills. They let him keep the handkerchief.

Now he sat, flanked by the two constables, in a bleak interview room, biting his fingernails. He kept quiet. His initial screams for help had dwindled into tears of frustration but now even crying was beyond him. He pulled his legs up till his heels rested on the seat of his chair, wrapped his arms around his knees and began to rock.

The constables looked up as Rossiter strode into the room, slammed a file of papers onto the desk that comprised the main furnishing of all the identical interview rooms and threw his bulky frame onto a lurid orange plastic chair.

"Okay, Simmons. Drugs."

Kit continued to rock.

"Sit up straight!" Rossiter ordered. "Put your feet down!"

Kit rocked.

One of the constables moved forwards.

"You heard the Inspector. Put your feet down."

The constable slapped Kit's knee to dislodge his feet from the chair but the drummer's pose remained rigid. His rocking increased. Rossiter frowned.

"Simmons, can you hear me?"

There was no reply.

"Shit!" Rossiter cursed.

"Do you think he needs a doctor?" the constable asked. "He doesn't look too good. Perhaps he's on something."

"Of course he is," spat back Rossiter. "What do you think I'm charging him with? Yeah, I guess you're right," his tone mellowed, "we'd better let a doctor have a look at him. Stick him in a cell and see who's on duty."

Rossiter rose, walked around the desk, grabbed a hank of Kit's hair and pulled his head backwards.

"You'd better not be pulling some kind of party trick, Simmons," he hissed.

As Rossiter let go, Kit's head dropped forwards like a rag doll. He started rocking again.

Kiesanowskis' breakfast table had become a council of war. Even as the police pulled out of Mike's driveway, Kelly had been dialling Sattherwaite on his cell phone. Sarah had been almost as prompt. After calming her two eldest children, placating and changing a wet, fractious baby then handing baby and bottle to an equally stressed husband, she had used the phone in the kitchen to call Kit's psychiatrist, Margaret Phillips who, in turn, had promised to call Kit's father, Keith Barrett.

Within thirty minutes a council of war had been convened. Kelly, like Mike still unshaven, reported that Sattherwaite would attend Kester at the police station within the hour. Margaret and Keith were still discarding coats and demanding details. Sarah was making frantic arrangements with her neighbour to baby-sit her children while Mike packed baby accoutrements into one of his wife's many voluminous carry bags. Jo made coffee. Mike explained as he packed.

"What do we do now?" Jo asked as he finished.

"Is there anything useful we can do?" Keith added.

"Practically, probably not," said Kelly, always logical. "Sattherwaite will do anything necessary."

"Well I can't just sit here doing nothing!" Jo attacked him. "I think we should go down to the station."

"What good would that do?" Kelly rejoined. "We won't be allowed in."

"I might be," Margaret interjected. "I am his doctor, after all."

"I think Jo's right," Keith added. "I can't sit here calmly drinking coffee knowing my son is stuck in some gaol cell.

Even if they don't let us in, at least I'll feel like I'm doing something. Hell, at least we might get to know what's going on."

"What about the kids?" Mike turned to his wife.

"No problem," she replied serenely. "Give me two minutes. I'll just pop them over next door. Come on girls!" she directed a call up the passage. "While I'm away," she returned her attention to her husband, "why don't you two men have a shave?"

Alone in a tiny cell, Kit curled himself up and resumed rocking. It was going to happen again and he didn't know why. He didn't know what he'd done but it must have been bad. They had promised him, after last time, that if he behaved himself he wouldn't have to go back, to go through it all over again. He had tried, honestly.

He tried to think what he might have done but he couldn't recall anything except vivid, terrifying images of last time. The prison cells were the same. The arrest had been the same, the search, the fingerprints, the photos, people shouting orders at him. The rest would be the same too. Nothing would stop it. Even Avi couldn't stop it last time.

And Avi wasn't even there now. He had already gone. He had always known Avi would go one day. He was much too clever to stay with anyone as stupid and useless as Kit. He'd always known he'd do something stupid enough to make Avi leave. Stupid enough or bad enough. It must have been something bad. Really bad.

Now he was back in here. In the little cells. They'd come soon and take him away. He'd be put into a van and taken to the other place, the one out in the country, the one with the bigger cells. The one with the other men. He rocked faster.

Breathing hard, his heart beat racing, Kit relived again the terrors of his previous prison sentence. Awake now, his brain replayed the horrific scenes it usually only recalled on the worst nights when the medication failed to work.

He remembered the huge rough men, the obscene gestures, the jeering threats of promised action. He recalled the cold, stainless steel washrooms, the group of huge men approaching. The guard, pushing him forwards and turning away, laughing at his fear, later ignoring his screams, later still taking his turn. As he rocked, he began to shake. The memories of the brutal gang rapes that had dominated his prison life flooded over him and Kit collapsed sideways onto the concrete slab bed, sobbing inconsolably.

The doctor watched silently. The young prisoner had been hunched and rocking when he had entered the small cell. Conversation had proved impossible. At first he had thought the young man was simply ignoring him but had rapidly decided that the prisoner was totally unaware of his presence. A touch to the man's shoulder had sent him into paroxysms of shaking. The doctor made some hurried notes on the clipboard he was carrying and knocked at the door to be released.

"Hi there!" The band and entourage swung as one at the cheery call.

"Nick! Hi!" Mike stepped forwards to grasp the newcomer's hand. "Nick Bennett from 'The Press'," he explained to the others.

Keith Barrett studied the scruffily-dressed reporter. So this was Nick Bennett. He had a lot to thank him for. Now was not the time.

"I thought I'd find you guys around here somewhere today," Bennett said happily. "Care to make my day with a few exclusive statements, Mike."

"Get stuffed, Nick!" Mike replied with a smile that removed the menace. "I don't suppose you know what's happening do you?"

"Probably no more than you do. I know they've arrested Kit and are charging him with possession of L.S.D.. He's due to appear in court in about half an hour. That's where I was heading. Rossiter isn't confirming it officially, but I hear he's going to charge him with Danny Gordon's murder as well."

"On what evidence?" Mike was outraged.

"Again, I didn't tell you this. Rossiter's not touting this around, but I hear they found the murder weapon with Kit's fingerprints all over it."

"But Kit wouldn't kill anyone," Sarah expostulated.

"Wouldn't he?" Nick asked, grinning wolfishly. "Look, I've probably known him longer than any of you. I went to school with him and Avi. We hung out together. The Beckenham Musketeers. I hate to tell you this but I think he's perfectly capable of killing someone. He's as nutty as a fruit cake. And if he was high on L.S.D., who knows? Anyway, I'm heading down to the courthouse. Coming?"

Kit's case was the fifth one called for the morning session. The group sat through an assortment of petty offences, tension rising. Nick grinned encouragement from the press bench. Then the court official called "Kester Joseph Simmons". Jo gasped.

Keith rose from his seat in concerned protest as Kit was

half-led, half-carried into the dock. Margaret Phillips put out a restraining hand. Keith sat.

Kit, unable to stand unattended, slumped onto the hard bench as soon as the police constable released his grasp. The magistrate's peremptory order to stand up was not so much unheeded as unheard. The prosecuting sergeant began a halting explanation.

"Has this man been seen by a doctor?" the magistrate broke in. "Is he fit to plead?"

"He has been seen, Sir, yes," the sergeant answered, speaking slowly as he riffled through his notes. "Ah, I have his report here, Sir."

The brief typed report was passed through the hands of several court officials as it made its way to the magistrate's bench. Sattherwaite leaned forwards and demanded his copy. The magistrate perused it rapidly.

"Does this man have counsel?" he asked, looking up.

"Yes, your Honour," replied Sattherwaite. "I have been so instructed."

"Ah, Mr Sattherwaite," the magistrate acknowledged. "Do you have any submissions on this matter?"

"Yes, Sir, I do," the lawyer stepped forwards grandly, straightening the lapels of his neat, grey suit in a habitual gesture. "It is my belief that the police are seeking a remand on this matter and will be opposing bail. I concur with the remand and submit that we will be entering a plea of 'not guilty' to all charges. However, on the matter of bail I would ask that the Court allows a submission from my client's psychiatrist, who is present in court. I believe her information on my client's medical history will explain several of the inconsistencies in the report you have just received."

Sattherwaite then passed through the system of officials a hand-written document, longer than the prison doctor's, which he and Margaret Phillips had hurriedly prepared during a brief discussion in the courthouse foyer. The magistrate re-read both documents unhurriedly. He turned to the prosecuting sergeant.

"Would the police have any objections to a remand to Sunnyside?"

"No, Sir."

"Very well. I think it could be the best thing under the circumstances." He picked up his gavel. "Kester Joseph Simmons, you are remanded to appear again in two weeks' time, date to be confirmed by the registrar. Bail is declined. You will be remanded in custody to Sunnyside Hospital for a psychiatric report." He slammed the gavel down.

Kit, still unaware of his surroundings, was led away.

"Oh, God, poor Kit," Sarah exclaimed as they re-assembled outside the courtroom. "He looks so sick."

"I want to know what they've done to him," Keith muttered angrily.

"Probably nothing," Margaret reassured him. "I suspected this might happen. Kit's view of the world is fairly fragile," she explained. "It doesn't take much to have it crash around him. Look, you people go home, there's nothing more you can do here. I'm going to try and stay with Kit. At least I can be at Sunnyside when he's brought in. I'll keep you posted," she promised as she left.

"Going to give me that exclusive comment now?" Nick Bennett inquired jauntily as he appeared from the courtroom.

Mike ran a hand despairingly through his long hair.

"Seriously? Okay, we're shocked and stunned. Oh, Nick it's bloody awful. What the hell do we do now?"

"Pass on a message for a start," Rossiter's voice broke in from behind. Mike turned.

"Tell that other musician buddy of yours I want to speak to him," Rossiter continued.

"Which other musician buddy? I have lots."

"Don't get smart. Your piano player. I want a word with him."

"So do we. He's missing."

"What?" both Rossiter and Bennett exclaimed in unison.

"Avi Livingstone is missing," Mike explained slowly. "None of us have seen him or heard from him since Thursday night, although Kit reckons he didn't leave him until yesterday morning. Said he was going home to change his clothes and hasn't been seen since."

"Hell!" Nick Bennett exclaimed. He hurried off, writing copy in his head as he ran.

At the gymnasium Danny's death was the main topic of conversation. In one corner a group of leotard-clad girls gossiped and cried while in another corner muscle-bound men took bets on who would win the national championship now Danny was out of the running. In the middle of the room a young man lifted weights and smiled to himself.

Cassandra Oakleigh had been thinking. The radio had announced Kester Simmons's arrest. He'd been sent to Sunnyside. That meant they thought he was crazy as well as guilty, even though the radio had broadcast an interview with some lawyer who'd insisted that Kester was pleading innocent, at least to the charge of murder. But Cassandra had no intention of letting them keep her Kester locked up. So she had been thinking.

After all, she knew something they didn't. She had watched him. Oh yeah, she knew who he was. She had seen him lots of times. She knew everyone who came to the little house. And where they went. She would have to be careful, though. It wasn't as if he would know who she was. He hadn't seen her. But he might want to know what she was doing so she would have to be very careful. Still, anything that helped Kester was a good thing so the danger didn't matter. It never occurred to her that this man had just killed and might be prepared to kill again.

Getting over to his house wasn't the difficult part. It was on the other side of town but the Orbiter bus was running so she could use it to get there and back. She prepared well, changing into black jeans and a black sweat shirt, stopping to admire herself in the mirror and to think how much Kester would admire her in black, then tying up her hair and hiding its striking red colour under a black woollen beanie.

At the bus stop she hopped anxiously from one foot to another, waiting for the bus which seemed to take much longer than usual to arrive. The driver punched her concession ticket without looking at her and she slunk unnoticed onto a seat at the back of the near-empty bus. Only two other passengers came and went before she reached a stop that she knew was only three blocks from her objective. The bus driver didn't acknowledge her as she alighted through the back door and walked purposefully away.

As she approached her destination she paused, suddenly doubting her ability to carry out her mission. What if she was caught? What would she say? How would she get away? Further down the road she spotted a small park with some children's play equipment. Determinedly keeping a steady pace, she walked right on past her destination to the park and sank heavily onto a swing, breathing hard.

She knew she had come too far to fail. Kester depended on her. There were two cars in the driveway as she had walked past so she would have to be at her most alert. Cassandra was very experienced at breaking and entering and knew exactly how to walk silently through houses while the inhabitants either slept soundly in their beds or worked in the kitchen as she moved. Most houses weren't as easy to break into as Kester's but most houses had better things to take. Things she could sell, or wear, or eat. She pulled herself off the swing and retraced her steps back down the street.

In reality, the action was easier than she expected. She had to be very careful, but it was fairly easy to slip into the toilet and hide until the coast was clear. She could hear a child complaining then a woman's voice answering, but they were in a room at the other end of the passage. She waited a moment longer then slipped quietly down the passage into the room she knew was his office. The filing cabinet in the corner was locked but the desk drawers weren't. She found the papers in the bottom drawer, in a large red folder. She didn't take them all, he might notice that. Just the important ones. The ones with Kester Simmons's name on them. And the big diagram.

Back outside, she thought again. Now she had the papers,

what should she do with them. She couldn't take them to the police. They would want to know how she got them and she couldn't tell them that. Cassandra paused under a large tree and thought harder. Then she took off at a run. The answer was obvious.

CHAPTER FIFTEEN

The hospital corridors were already buzzing with the day's activities when Elizabeth arrived. She found her son sitting up in bed, attempting to grin through the livid bruised swelling that made up most of his face.

"I'm sorry I'm a bit late, dear," Elizabeth began, stooping to kiss her son carefully on the cheek. "I slept in."

"Hey, it's okay. You're entitled. I'm just waiting for the doctor. I believe they're going to let me out."

"I thought they might. I brought you some clean clothes." She placed an overnight bag on the end of his bed. Avi checked the contents then looked at his mother incredulously.

"How did you get these? Did you go back home?"

"No," his mother shook her head, laughing lightly. "I'm not that stupid." Her tone darkened. "All that time when you were shut in that hell hole yesterday and your father was sitting in his armchair demanding to be fed, I managed to sneak a few things into your car. Not much, some clothes, your passport, your glasses," she grinned conspiratorially, "your keyboard."

"My keyboard?" Avi was all admiration. "You got my keyboard? Mum, you're wonderful!"

"Well," she shrugged. "I know you keep one over where you practise, but you saved hard for that one. It's got a nice tone."

Avi laughed and gave his mother a one-handed hug. She knew him well.

"I don't disapprove," she said, pulling away. "Of you and,

ah, Kester," She spoke hesitantly. "I don't understand, but I don't disapprove. It's your life. You've always been a sensible boy. If you've really thought about this and it's the right thing for you, then how could I disapprove. I want you to be happy. You have thought about it, haven't you?"

"Mum, Dad had it all wrong. I'm not gay. Kit is, we both know that, but I'm not. We really are just good friends. Sure, I've thought about it. Hey, I'll even admit we've tried, you know, getting it together. Kit wanted it. But it wasn't my thing and we decided we had been friends too long ever to make good lovers." He gave her a lop-sided smile. "We've slept together twice, that's all." He shrugged resignedly. "You never know though, it might have worked if I'd been that way inclined. After all we've known each other eighteen years and we haven't had a serious argument yet. That's got to count for something."

His mother didn't smile back. Rubbing her hands together thoughtfully, she looked him in the eye.

"Avrahim," she said quietly. "You're very like your father in some ways. You like to be in control of things. I think your Kester is like me, the submissive type. He won't argue." She leant forwards and grasped Avi's good hand. "You've got a lot of control over that young man. Don't abuse it."

"Never, Mum. Never."

Two nurses rattled a trolley through the door.

"Isn't it awful about 'Charlotte Jane'," Avi heard one of them say.

"Yeah. Just before a tour, too. I had tickets."

"I was listening to the radio before. Did you know they've arrested the drummer."

Avi could contain himself no longer.

"Excuse me," he called out. "What about 'Charlotte Jane'?"

"The lead singer's been killed," the first nurse supplied.

"Yeah, and the drummer's been arrested," added the second. "It's all in the paper."

She fished a 'Press' from the trolley's shelf and passed it to Avi. The headlines glared at him from the front page - the main story, by-lined Dominic Bennett, accompanied by a quarter-page coloured picture of Danny's body being carried out on a stretcher. Avi read the article in silence and turned to his mother.

"I've got to get out of here. Right now." He called to the nurses, "How do I sign myself out of here?"

The first nurse walked calmly over to his bed.

"I believe you're going to be discharged as soon as the doctor has seen you."

"I don't give a toss about the doctor," Avi snapped. "I want to go now."

"What's the problem?"

"This!" Avi pointed to the newspaper. "I've got to go."

He hauled himself out of bed and began to draw the curtains around it so he could get dressed. His mother stepped outside, drew the nurse with her and explained rapidly. The nurse nodded her understanding and dashed off to find somebody more official.

Fifteen minutes later they were outside the hospital. Elizabeth surveyed her son, pale beneath the bruising and swaying slightly, and wondered if she should have insisted he stay. It would have been futile. Resigned, she unlocked the car, coaxed it into starting and pulled out of the grounds into the heavy Riccarton Avenue traffic.

"Where to?"

"Kit's."

"How do we get there. I'm not used to this side of town. You navigate, I'll drive."

"Oh, what a pretty little place," Elizabeth exclaimed as they drew up outside the Avon Loop cottage. "It's so quaint."

Avi leapt from the car, only to be stopped by a policeman. They exchanged a few words and Avi climbed back into the passenger's seat, muttering darkly.

"There's nobody here," he explained. "It's sealed off. Let's try Mike's."

"Just point the way."

The journey from the Avon Loop to Riccarton traversed half of the city, down some of its busiest roads. Elizabeth was becoming a proficient city driver very quickly.

"This is a bit naughty, really," she commented, deftly swinging the car across lanes.

"What?"

"Driving on a Saturday. Your father would never approve."

"So who's asking him? Anyway, saving life overrides all rules."

"Whose life? It's too late for Danny."

"Kit's," Avi answered flatly.

The Riccarton address was empty. Avi thumped his good hand hard onto his car bonnet in frustration, then winced as the action sent a wave of pain through his body.

"Take it easy," his mother called from the driver's seat. "We'll find them. Joanna's, maybe?"

"Nah! Unlikely. Anyway, they'll all be at Chapel." He sighed. "Bennett!" he exclaimed, climbing back into the car. "Nick Bennett. We'll try him. At least he might know what's going on. Press building, Cathedral Square."

With a shrug of resignation, Elizabeth began the reverse journey.

"We should have foreseen this with your father," she said as she drove. "You should have got out years ago."

"And left you to face the consequences? I couldn't."

"Oh, Avrahim," she laughed sadly. "I only stayed for you. We should have talked."

"Nick's not back yet," the girl said, checking her watch. "He shouldn't be long." She studied Avi's wounded face. "Tell you what, wait here. I'll bring you a coffee."

Avi and Elizabeth sank into the proffered chairs, gratefully accepting the foam cups presented by the young reporter. They didn't have to wait long. Before the coffee was cool enough to drink a whirlwind of energy exploded into the newsroom. Nick stopped in his tracks at the sight of his school friend.

"Avrahim! Everybody's looking for you!"

"Yeah, I thought they might be. I'm looking for them. What the hell's going on?"

"Start by telling me where you've been," Nick demanded, settling himself beside them and helping himself to Avi's coffee.

Avi rescued his coffee and explained, listening in turn to Nick's record of events.

"So," Nick concluded, "I've just come steaming down here with this amazing scoop about the missing Avrahim and he's camped in my office. The others have headed back to Mike's place. They should be there soon."

"They can wait. I'm more concerned with Kit. He didn't kill Danny Gordon. I know he didn't. Damn it, I was with him all night."

"Then let's start with Rossiter." Nick reached for a phone and dialled the police number from memory. "Inspector Rossiter," he began as he was finally connected, "Nick Bennett."

"I don't have any more information for you," Rossiter snarled into the receiver.

"Maybe not," Nick responded cheerfully, "but I have some for you."

Brian Rossiter put down the receiver and scowled at the constable who stood quietly waiting.

"So what have you got there?" the inspector demanded.

"A report that came in on Thursday, Sir," Rikki Merata replied. "It's relevant to the 'Charlotte Jane' thing."

Rossiter scanned the pages.

"Why didn't I see this before?" he demanded.

"I don't know, Sir. I've just come back on duty. I didn't hear about Danny Gordon until this morning. I've been in Amberley cooking mussels with my cousin who has a racehorse," he finished lamely.

Margaret Phillips met Avi in a corridor of Sunnyside Hospital, taking in his appearance without comment.

"Rossiter has cleared everything," she began. "The murder charge has been dropped and they've agreed to bail on the possession one. Keith has sorted that. But I don't know if he can go home, Avi. He's just not responding. Even I can't get through.”

She led Avi into a small, pleasantly decorated room.

“He just sits and rocks. He doesn't even know we're here. I've tried everything, but...,” she shrugged.

“Let me try,” Avi smiled lopsidedly.

Avi pulled a chair directly in front of the one on which Kit was rocking compulsively. Carefully manoeuvring his broken hand, Avi put his arms around Kit till he held him tight and began to rock in synchronisation. Imperceptibly, he changed the rhythm of the rocking to a more gentle pace. He could feel Kit relaxing in his arms until, finally, the drummer came to his senses, recognised his friend, tightened his grip and buried his face in Avi's neck. Avi looked up and winked at the psychiatrist.

“We're going home,” he said quietly.

“I still don't know how you did that,” Margaret asked admiringly.

“Piece of cake,” Avi replied smugly, settling back on Mike's couch. “You just have to remember Kit isn't human, he's a walking drum kit, he does everything to a drum beat. I've even seen him tap out a cigarette in a swing rhythm.”

Keith laughed. Avi continued.

“So it was simple. All I did was reprogram the beat. The brain was bound to notice sooner or later.”

“If neither of you two killed Danny, who did?” Jo interjected over the laughter.

“I don't know, but I might have heard them,” said Avi. “About ten I heard footsteps. I thought it might be whoever had been bugging Kit, so I got up to check. All I got for my trouble was an obscene ear bashing from Danny who had obviously come back to fix the amp, although I reckon he was pretty drunk. About an hour later, Kit was asleep, I heard more footsteps. I assumed it was Danny leaving. I didn't need another shouting match, so I ignored it. If Danny didn't leave, it must have been whoever killed him. I wish I'd looked now."

"Just as well you didn't. You might be dead too," Keith pointed out practically.

"I think we should eat," broke in Sarah. "Avi, can you and Elizabeth eat chicken with salad?"

"Yeah, absolutely," Avi explained. "I'm not sure about Kelly, though, He's vegetarian."

"Oh dear! Kelly?"

Kelly turned from the photo he had been studying.

"Sorry, I wasn't listening. Michael, when was this taken?"

"Three years ago. Why?"

"Have you got any other crowd shots?"

"Yeah, heaps."

"Can I see them?"

Mike pulled a bulging album from a bookcase by the television.

"What are you looking for?"

Kelly didn't reply until he had four different shots lying on the coffee table in front of them.

"Look," He pointed to a figure with red hair, always in the same place at the foot of the stage. "By the dates on the back these photos cover five years. Same girl." He paused, timing his revelation for dramatic effect. "Is this not the very same redhead who attacked Kester so lasciviously in the bread shop?" Kelly watched the news sink in. "She knows where you live, Kester. She came on Thursday, while you were indisposed. I turned her away."

Nick helped himself to Avi's coffee again.

"Rossiter thinks it's all got to do with drugs," he said between gulps. "Danny Gordon was chock full of steroids and Rossiter reckons Kit must have been supplying them."

"Steroids? Where the hell would I get those?" Kit exploded.

"Don't shoot the messenger," Nick placated him. "I'm just passing on what I heard from Rossiter."

"Why would Danny take steroids?" inquired Keith, who hadn't known him.

"Instant muscles," Nick supplied. "He was a competitive body builder, wasn't he?"

"Yes," Sarah agreed. "With an important competition just after the tour ended. Remember, Mike, he was telling me about it. It sounded as if it was very important to him to win."

"Instant muscles! Of course!" Jo exclaimed. "Those packets he made up for lunch. Instant-muscles-just-add-water. I used to tease him about it until he started to throw those hissy fits."

"A bit bolshy, was he?" Nick asked.

"Tell us about it!" Avi answered. "I was telling Jo the other day, Danny was quite a nice bloke when we first met him. He got argumentative after he started doing all that weight training. In the last few weeks he's been positively bloody violent!"

"Steroids'll do that. At least, so I've heard. One of my colleagues in the sports department was doing an article about a support group being organised for body builders' wives. Apparently they can get really hyped up on the things and from what I gather the stuff Danny was taking was a pretty high-powered little cocktail."

Kit, who had been rocking gently to himself and had not appeared to be taking any interest in the conversation, leant forwards suddenly.

"If Danny was on drugs and drunk, like Avi said, he might have killed himself," he suggested.

"Nah, I doubt it," Avi disagreed. "Too much ego."

"Too many stab wounds," added Nick.

CHAPTER SIXTEEN

"The children are asleep," Sarah reported thankfully. She glanced around the room, which was beginning to look like an airport transit lounge, empty coffee mugs and dirty plates strewn in all directions. Nobody had shown any inclination to leave and she had been secretly worried that they were settling in for a second night, so she was relieved when Avi took the hint, announcing that he wasn't feeling well and needed sleep too.

Kit's enquiry about where he should go as he couldn't go home was answered by Elizabeth who suggested he join her and Avi at her motel and Elizabeth readily agreed with Margaret Phillip's suggestion that she go with them to check on Kit and organise some pain relief for Avi. In a matter of minutes Kelly had organised a taxi for himself and Jo, Nick had offered Keith a ride into the central city and Sarah was left to restore her lounge. She closed the door as the others left, leant back against it and let out a heartfelt sigh. Mike nodded in agreement.

"Let me guess. Wishing they would all go home then feeling guilty for thinking that? Me too. I'll give you a hand to get this mess cleaned up."

Outside, as Elizabeth unlocked Avi's car, she noticed a small piece of paper tucked under the windshield. She pulled it out, read it, exclaimed with surprise then handed the paper to Avi who squinted at it through his blackened eye and bent glasses before passing it on to Kit to read out.

"Meet me in Barbadoes St cemetery, opposite Kester's house, asap. urgent. Cassandra."

"Cassandra?" Avi thought hard. "That's the redhead fan, yeah?"

"Yeah, should we go?"

"It could be a trap," Elizabeth worried.

"Could be, but we won't know until we go," Avi replied.

"All of us?"

"No, Mum. Hey Nick! Keith!" Avi shouted to get the attention of the two men who were heading to a car further down the street. "Mum, you take Dr Phillips and Kit to the motel. I'll take Nick and Keith to meet this girl. Safety in numbers."

"Are you sure you're okay to go?" Margaret Phillips queried.

"Yeah. Tired, sore, hurt everywhere, but this could be important. We won't be long and Nick can drive."

"Why did she put the note on the car?" Kit asked. "Why didn't she knock on the door?"

She was easy to find. Perched on the top of a large, granite tombstone, Cassandra looked like a live version of a carved angel, her hair flowing in waves over the back of her denim jacket. As the three men approached she jumped off the tombstone, pulled her jacket tight across her bosom and tried to look demure.

"I thought Kit should know," she blurted out without preamble. "I saw the dude."

"What dude?" Nick prompted.

"On Thursday. You all came and went so much. I saw you," she pointed to Avi, "and the girl and the lady. And you all left and Kester looked so sick and I saw Danny and I saw the dude in the track suit. The jogger."

"You mean Kelly?" Avi queried, wondering where her rapid-fire speech was leading.

"Who's he?"

"Short, spiky hair, carries a bass guitar."

"No, not him," she turned on him scathingly. "I said the dude, not the yuppie."

"I'm not with you, then. What dude?"

"Are you telling us you saw the person who killed Danny Gordon?" Nick interjected.

"Yeah, that's what I'm trying to tell you! It was the dude in the tracksuit. I've seen him lots of times. He drives a sports car. Parks it around by the hotel and jogs around to Kester's house. I saw him on Thursday. Come and go. Then he came back. I know where he works," Cass held out some pieces of paper. "I took this from his office."

Avi stared at the paper until the blurs made sense. "Oh my God!" he breathed, before passing the paper to Keith.

"Bloody hell!" Keith turned the pages over several times, barely believing what he was reading. "Bloody Hell!"

"What is it?" Nick asked anxiously.

"Dynamite," Keith replied.

"We need to show these to Rossiter," Avi suggested. "I'll call him."

"Wait!" Keith stopped him as he read the document again. "The bastard'll just deny it. This may give him a motive but it doesn't prove him guilty, even with this young lady as a witness. We need more."

"How?"

Oh, I think there could be a way." He smiled maliciously. "Nick, do you have a voice recorder?"

"Of course."

"Good. Before that, though, we need to make copies of these then, I hate to say it, we need to get these originals back where they came from before he notices. Can you do that, Cassandra?"

Cass pulled her jacket tighter, shivering at the idea, but nodded bravely. "If I have to."

"To the Press building then," Nick ordered. "Three copies of these. One for you to show Kit, one for Rossiter, who doesn't need to know how we got them, and one for me for my exclusive feature article when they nail him."

Nick and Cass approached like a well-rehearsed tag-team. Nick introduced himself as a reporter and indicated that Cass was there to take photographs for the article. Cass held up Nick's camera, smiled and said nothing. The bluff worked. They were led into the office where, while Cass randomly pointed the camera and hoped she looked like she knew what she was doing, Nick explained that he wanted a formal interview that he could quote in the paper, then asked a variety of questions before giving a polite "thank you" and standing to leave. As he walked his interviewee back down the passage to the entrance, Cass grabbed her chance, quickly opening the drawer, thrusting the papers back into the red folder and slamming the drawer shut before innocently joining Nick as he stretched out his goodbyes to give her enough time.

"That was too scary!" Cass expelled a relieved sigh as they sank into the safety of Nick's car.

"High five!" Nick offered out his upraised hand.

Rossiter was not impressed at being called back to work.

"This had better be worth it, John," he complained as he walked into the office. "What's this new evidence?"

John Matheson handed Rossiter the copied papers. Rossiter skimmed through them and whistled softly. "Where did you get these?"

"Those two," he indicated through a window in the wall to Avi and Keith who were sitting in an adjoining room. "The older one is Simmons's father, he wants to talk to you."

"Wheel him in then."

The young man smiled at his reflection in the full-length mirror. He flexed his body in a variety of poses, admiring the bulging of the muscles, the lines of the veins. Now everything he wanted was at his fingertips. There was no-one, now, to stand in his way. He smiled again, satisfied.

Mike, too, felt satisfied. The situation had remedied itself quite nicely. Messy but convenient. He felt a bit guilty about what he had planned, but not too guilty. In the end, it had been a business decision. Nothing personal. Okay, it was personal, but the solution was business. Mike liked contracts.

"Good evening, Sir," Keith rose from the vinyl chair and offered his business card. "Keith Barrett. I hope I haven't called at too inconvenient a time, but I am on a very tight schedule. My good friend suggested I meet with you," he continued, quoting the name he had read on the document and using all the right business executive jargon.

"Come this way," his companion said. "We'll talk in my

office."

"I'm in antiques," Keith continued as they settled into the office chairs, broadening his American twang for the occasion. "I've got money and I'm looking to invest some in your country. They told me you had a project running. Something about real estate?"

"Town houses," the younger man smiled. "My partner and I will be building designer town houses. Top class section."

"How soon?" Keith inquired.

The younger man smiled again, coldly.

"I predict the property's present dwelling, an old house, should be demolished within the next three months. Construction will begin immediately after that."

"And this section belongs to you and your partner?" Keith smiled back.

"It will. Very soon."

"My research says the property is still occupied. I assume your profit margin has taken the purchase price into account?"

The young man laughed.

"There is no purchase price. Look, I'll be honest. The land belongs to our family. My brother lives in the house at the moment but, between you and me, he's quite mad. My mother and I are arranging to have him committed. He won't need the house any more."

Keith restrained his welling anger.

"I gather your mother is your partner in this venture?" he asked levelly.

"Yes," Gabriel Simmons concurred. "She's in real estate. I say, if you're in antiques, you might like to look over the place before we pull it down. You might like some of the furniture."

"So let me get this straight," Keith recapped. "You and your mother have arranged to commit your brother to a mental asylum. Then you plan to sell the back of the section to the supermarket developers and build town houses on the front. Correct?"

"Correct."

"So why did you kill the guitarist?"

Gabriel turned pale.

"I don't know what you're talking about," he bluffed.

"You were seen," Keith's teeth parted in an evil grin.

"Rubbish! There was no-one...," Gabriel stopped, realising what he had just said, then sighed in defeat before delivering one last defiant shot. "Even if he did see anything, Kester would have been so stoned on those drugs his testimony will be useless."

"It wasn't Kester." Brian Rossiter stepped through the door. "It was someone else. A very astute, very credible witness who has given an excellent statement, listing every time she has seen you at your brother's house. Why did you kill the guitarist?"

"So why did he kill Danny?" Jo still didn't understand.

"It was an accident," Keith explained over a late Sunday brunch at Elizabeth's motel. "They wanted the land. It's worth a lot of money. His intention was merely to drive Kester crazy, so he could be committed."

"That would give Mum and Gabriel complete power of attorney and they could sell the place out from under me," Kit finished between bites of toast.

"It was Gabriel making the malicious phone calls, to break

Kit's sleep pattern. Along with the hallucinogens amongst his tablets, it was scrambling Kit quite successfully."

"On top of that," Kit took up the story again, ticking the items off on his fingers as he spoke, "he got into my house while I was out, or asleep, lots of times, and moved things around, so I'd think I was going crazy, which I did. He also cut back my money so I was half starved, which made the L.S.D. work even better and they fed me all that crap about being too stupid to handle my own money, which I believed because he's a doctor and I've got the self-esteem of a dead gnat." He grinned sheepishly at Margaret Phillips who had joined them for breakfast.

"Why go to all that trouble?" Jo asked. "He's a doctor. If he wanted you committed, couldn't he have just put you away?"

"No," Margaret broke in. "They needed my signature, and one of my colleagues at Sunnyside. And I've treated Kit for too long to be fooled. They needed to create some genuine psychosis symptoms. I don't mind telling you, Kit, they nearly succeeded. I was getting very worried about you."

"So let me get this straight," Jo proceeded. "Danny came back on Thursday night to fix the amp. Why was Gabriel there?"

"To slash my drums," Kit replied. "He knew the fuss he had caused with Gary's bass guitar. He did that. He was running out of time. The supermarket wanted the land fast and once we had left on tour he wouldn't have been able to harass me. I would have come right. He had to finish me off before we left. So he thought he would really wind me up by slashing my drums. If I'd thought I had done that without knowing, I would have committed myself." Kit took another bite of his toast before continuing. "Apparently, he didn't see Danny, who was down behind the amps. Danny heard him and watched for a while. Then, when he realised what Gabriel was doing, he leapt out to stop him and Gabriel stabbed him. He died trying to save my drums."

'Charlotte Jane' surveyed the rehearsal room. The blood was still on the floor. Kit scuffed it with his boot.

"I guess the tour's off," Avi said grimly. "No guitarist, no keyboards," He indicated his sling.

"No keyboards!" Jo exclaimed indignantly. "Oh yeah?" She marched over to the Roland, still on its stand, turned it on, played one of Avi's more complex melodies and smiled at her cousin benignly. "You're not the only pianist in the family, you know."

"So, we still need a guitar," Avi protested.

"And drums," Kit added. "These are not going to sound so good."

"Defeatists," Mike mocked. "It's simple. Avi does vocals. Jo takes over Avi's keyboard and Pete'll play lead guitar."

"Pete?" Avi looked incredulous. "Pete Branston?"

"The very same. He should be flying in later today. He was coming anyway. I'd already been onto him about Danny's contract and Pete thought he'd come up with a way to break it."

"So he was the hitman you mentioned the other day," Jo said with relief.

"Yeah."

"Why did I have to keep it secret?"

"Because I didn't want Danny to get any hint of it. We were trying to fire him, after all."

"So we have a band," Jo enthused.

"We still need drums," Kit reminded her.

"Take a look in there," Mike indicated a large cardboard box stacked behind the door. "It arrived from Tama this morning, special delivery. Replacement parts."

He grinned as Kit fell delightedly on the box and began ripping it open.

"So," asked Jo excitedly. "Do we tour?"

"Say, Kelly," Kit looked up. "If we are going on tour, can I borrow your hot pink t-shirt?"

Other books by J.L. O'Rourke

Deep in the Shallows
A Lake Waihola Mystery

Andrea North sees a job at beautiful Lake Waihola as a welcome escape from her controlling ex, but an easy task is soon complicated by a strange hoard and a close encounter with an arrogant pig hunter. When the campground dog pulls a gruesome object from the lake, Andy must decide who is she fighting against and who she can trust.

Blood in the Wings
The First of Severn

Vampires and murder backstage in a Christchurch theatre. 16 year old Riley Lowe is working as a stage hand, backstage at her theatre company's annual show. Her classmate from school, Tasha, is also in the show as a dancer and, as usual, she is flirting with all the guys. In particular, she is trying to take the one Riley is attracted to. Severn is one of a group of professional theatre crew who are helping with the show but the closer she gets to him, the more Riley realises that there is something strange about the group who live and work in the dark. When Tasha is killed and Severn disappears, Riley learns their terrible secret. But can she solve the murder in time to save Severn?

About the Author

J. L. O'Rourke has worked as a journalist, sub-editor, free-lance writer and office administrator. When not writing, she enjoys being in a theatre, either onstage as a singer or backstage where she has been everything from floor crew to stage-manager. She lives in Christchurch, New Zealand.

www.ingramcontent.com/pod-product-compliance
Lightning Source LLC
Chambersburg PA
CBHW051047050726
47592CB00002B/425

Learning Places: *Genuine Peace*

This book is an attempt to capture some of the key aspects of the very complex subject of peace, in a highly summarized, easily understandable and practically usable form.

The topics, issues, methods and approaches described here have sought to be directly relevant and central to the theme and goal of describing and achieving a pure, beneficial and effective form of peace (genuine peace).

In the interest of efficiency and to minimize the size of manuscript, I have not had space to tell many anecdotal background stories but have nevertheless sought to provide sufficient detail for readers to understand each area being discussed and the principles and learning which are espoused.

Please join me on this quest for *genuine peace.*

Kindest Regards,
David Apelt

Acknowledgements

In writing this book I would like to thank: Mum who always told me I could do whatever I set my heart upon, and who always demonstrated her love and faithfulness through words of affirmation and in the way she gave herself tirelessly to her husband, her marriage, her children and the numerous family endeavours which we explored together; Dad who, being a man of few words showed his love through his actions in seeking to care and provide for our family. My father demonstrated that if you live and work faithfully and responsibly in life you will achieve your dreams; June my beautiful, gifted, capable, intuitive, creative, loving, wonderful first wife who shared thirty six delightful and fulfilling years of marriage with me, before going home to glory; Kathy my beautiful, talented, capable, erudite, insightful, thoughtful, learned, loving second wife who is God's wonderful gift to me that we might also fulfill His Divine purposes in this next chapter of our lives together; Then there are all of our amazingly clever gifted and legendary children and grandchildren who have brought us such joy and taught us so much; and finally our innumerable other influential friends, family, colleagues and acquaintances in life and work.

There are so many who have gone before and journeyed with us in this rich and eventful lifetime, as well as demonstrated that everyone matters, and we can each make a very real difference in this world.

Thank You One and All.